Donated to the
Library by

Top Ladies
of Distinction, Inc.

Michigan Metro
Chapter

J FIC

THE KATURRAN ODYSSEY

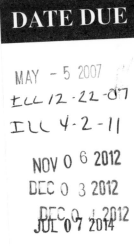

THE KATURRAN ODYSSEY

Book One – Finding Home

CREATED AND ILLUSTRATED BY TERRYL WHITLATCH
WRITTEN BY DAVID MICHAEL WIEGER
EDITED BY ELLEN STEIBER
DIGITAL COLORING BY TERRYL WHITLATCH & STEPHANIE LOSTIMOLO

AN IMAGINOSIS BOOK

SIMON & SCHUSTER
NEW YORK   LONDON   TORONTO   SYDNEY

Prologue
ANOTHER TIME

It is said, in some far and distant lands, that speaking the name of a place connects you to its heart and can breathe it into being. *Bo-hibba.* Within the song of the word is the scent of ripe fruit and vanilla and the fertile musk of a jungle. Can you smell it? *Bo-hibba.* Can you hear the high-pitched call of parrots and the faint crackle of long grasses drying in the sun?

Bo-hibba. An island floating in a vast sea, alone in the waters of the world. And on this island is a village called Kattakuk. And in this village, there is one who changed the lives of all who lived there then and all who live there now. *Bo-hibba.* Say it out loud and breathe it into being . . . *Bo-hibba.*

On a day when the sun sent dusty spears of light slashing through the majestic baobab trees, lemur kits gathered gifts for the storyteller who had just arrived from his secret home in the darkest part of the jungle. They collected bunches of sweet bananas—short as a nose, thick as a tail—and baskets of plump berries. And the gift of all gifts: fat black figs, so ripe they were arranged on beds of soft grass so they would not burst open in a wonderful, gooey mess.

These gifts were piled in the cool shade of the huge baobab in the center of the lemur village. Then the young lemurs raced to sit as close as possible to the storyteller. Though his eyes were closed, they all knew he was waiting for the quiet that comes only when excited kits are listening very carefully.

After a long pause, he began: "In a time many seasons past, lived a young lemur. He was smaller than most but more courageous than many. His name was Katook.

"Life changed forever on Bo-hibba because of what Katook saw and what he did, but most importantly because of how he followed the calling in his heart to bring about a miracle that ended the Long Winter. If not for Katook, none of us would be here now, safe and warm in this tree with our bellies full of sweet figs.

"Was Katook chosen for his adventure, or did his adventure choose him? Only the great Fossah knows. What I know is that Katook began hungry and shivering with cold, just like all the other lemurs on Bo-hibba. But I'm getting ahead of myself. Close your eyes. I will tell you the story of the Long Winter . . .

1

Chapter One
HOME

It had never been this dark and cold in Kattakuk. The sky was stone gray and the cold so bitter that it made Katook's teeth chatter. He and his family huddled in their wicker home high in the treetops. He could feel it swaying wildly in the howling gale outside.

Restless and bored, Katook opened a window latch and peered outside at the bare fig trees and the brittle, dry leaves blowing across the forest floor. He missed the joy of leaping from one tree to another. He missed wrestling for hours with his best friend, Naxo. He missed the smell of sweet summer grass. And he missed falling asleep with the sun warming his fur.

Since both the sun and moon were hidden behind the heavy clouds, it was impossible to know exactly how long it had been since winter had settled on Bo-hibba and held them all captive in their basket homes. He thought it could have been for five full moon-treads, though it felt more like ten.

Katook's empty belly rumbled. Oh, how he longed to see sunshine dance on the wide green fig leaves again. And to see ripe figs tucked under the leaves like secret treasures. *Stop it*, Katook told himself. Thinking about figs just made the ache in his belly worse. It was better to think of other things.

Katook carefully shut the window, then rolled onto his back. He closed his eyes and listened to the sound of the wind tearing through the trees.

"Watch out!" Kai, his younger brother, landed on his belly, knocking the wind out of him.

Kai was a pest, but Katook knew that his brother was as hungry and scared as he was. He tossed Kai into the air and caught him on the soft fur of his belly, causing squeals of delight. "Shhh," whispered Katook, gesturing toward their sister. "Lina's sleeping."

"Again!" insisted Kai. "Higher! I'll be quiet."

2

As Katook lifted his brother, he heard his parents' voices. Though he couldn't make out their words, he could tell that something was wrong. He set Kai down then silently started toward the doorway.

He heard his mother, Oola, say, "An offering of figs has always pleased the great Fossah in the past. Surely it will work again." Her voice sounded frightened and unsure.

"But, my love," Katook's father, Hano, replied sadly, "if we give the few figs we have to the Fossah, we'll have nothing left for ourselves."

Katook and Kai watched their parents bow low on the ground and begin to pray.

"Oh, great Fossah, powerful Lord of the Land and Sky, we don't know what we did to displease you, but we ask that you forgive us and return the sun and the rains to Bo-hibba. We ask that you remember us and warm us in your light, as you have for so many seasons. Without the sun and the rains, great Fossah, there will be no figs on the trees, and we will all die of hunger."

Katook quietly pulled Kai away from the doorway. "We'll be all right, let's go to sleep."

Katook dreamed that the gray sky cracked open and golden sunlight drenched the village in warmth.

On the first day of the new moon, just before darkness fell, Gamic, the High Priest of the great Fossah, rang the temple's chimes.

Then eerie, high-pitched moans joined in an unearthly chorus, summoning all the lemurs of Bo-hibba to the temple.

Katook slowly rose from his bed of grass. He licked his paw and smoothed the tuft of fur that he knew would be poking straight up behind his left ear. He found his mother staring sadly into the family's food basket.

"Oh, Mother," Katook said as he hurried to her side. "It will be full again in no time."

"You're right. No time at all," she said with forced cheerfulness.

But before Katook could find words to comfort her, his father called out, "It's time."

Katook hoisted a sleeping Kai into his arms and followed his father outside into the freezing wind. Oola and Lina climbed down after them, joining the other lemur families as they, too, obeyed the High Priest's call.

As they moved far from the safety of their homes high in the trees, they became keenly aware of the beasts that came out only in the dark, and were as hungry as they were.

The lemurs had to make their way down a long, narrow path on the edge of a cliff that fell away into a dark swath of jungle. This place was called the Forbidden Trees—an area that the priests forbade anyone other than themselves to enter.

5

Katook couldn't resist staring down into the trees. Their leaves were so thick that he couldn't even glimpse the jungle floor. It was said that light never touched the ground there, and that the earth was darker than a moonless night sky.

His mother nudged him along, and the path opened onto a vast field of dry grass. Rising up in the middle of this Gathering Place was the temple, a long-dead baobab tree, twisted and blackened from age, its branches spiking high into the sky. It was here that the old lemur Gamic, his priests, and their Indrii temple guards lived and worshiped the Fossah. A steep stone stairway led up to a rusted metal door in the center of the tree's twisted trunk. Only Gamic, the High Priest, was allowed to pass through it.

Katook tried not to tremble. Everything connected with the Fossah was frightening, but none more so than the temple. His eyes were drawn to the round stone platform and the wicker basket on top of it. A line of masked priests, each one holding a torch, circled the basket. Behind them, in a larger circle, Indriis stood at attention, their arms crossed over their massive chests. Hand-chosen by Gamic, they were raised apart from the community to be the protectors of all things sacred. They were larger and stronger than most lemurs, both brave and fiercely loyal. And it was their unworldly voices that had summoned the lemurs, who now formed a long line in front of the platform.

A new, high-pitched chime rang. Then the lemurs left their offerings in the wicker baskets.

Katook climbed onto the stone platform. He circled his tail overhead twice, as was the custom, then approached the Fossah's basket. Looking into it, he saw it was barely filled with figs. Clearly, few families were able to give more than a single fruit. Most had nothing to give at all.

Katook unclenched his paw and stared at his shriveled fig. He was tempted to eat the offering himself, but he knew that was the gravest wrong. He quickly dropped it into the basket.

Taking a place beside his father, Katook knelt on the frozen grass and held his paws over his eyes. He wrapped his tail around his chest for warmth, but it didn't do much good.

"Father," he whispered, "what are we waiting for?"

"For Gamic, the High Priest, to appear and lead us in a prayer for the sun's return."

"What if that doesn't work?"

Hano was silent a moment, then whispered, "Are you old enough to know the truth, Katook?"

"Yes, Father," Katook answered, wondering as he said it if it was true.

"Perhaps you are. Very well. Unless the sun and rains return before the third new moon, we will all die."

Katook stared at his father, wishing he had never asked the question.

Darkness gathered in the shadows of the trees. The lemurs waited patiently for Gamic. In seasons past this had been a festive time, with music and dancing and a great feast to celebrate the earth's renewal. But this year there was little to celebrate, and the lemurs shivered as they prayed to the Great One, Lord of Light and Dark, Giver and Taker of All Things, more terrible than the Cold, more generous than the Trees, more powerful than the Wind. Whatever it was that they'd done wrong, they would beg for the Fossah's forgiveness.

Finally, Katook heard the moan of grinding on metal. Katook knew it was forbidden to steal even a glance at the High Priest, but he couldn't resist. He peered through his paws and saw the largest and most ferocious of the Indrii guards drag open the heavy temple door. The guard had coarse black fur and a long, shiny scar carved from brow to chin.

Katook knew that this guard's name was Reet. It was said that Reet's mighty arms could crush you like a blossom, and that his heart was colder than death itself.

Katook heard a sputtering flame and smelled strong incense. From out of the blackest shadow inside the old baobab tree stepped Gamic, the High Priest of all of Bo-hibba. He wore a purple cape and a magnificent mask of orange mud and flame-blue parrot feathers. His ruby-studded tail glittered in the torchlight. He was neither tall, nor particularly well built, but he had an air of authority that set him apart. He was the lemurs' messenger to the Fossah, their last and only hope.

One of the priests handed Gamic a torch. Gamic clasped it in both paws and slowly descended the stairs.

The High Priest moved through the kneeling, shivering villagers and gently placed one lemur's tail on another's. At first this laying on of tails seemed random, but Katook soon realized that Gamic was creating a circle, connecting every lemur on Bo-hibba to every other.

Katook heard the High Priest drawing near and quickly closed his eyes. He shivered as he felt Gamic's spidery fingers place his tail on his mother's. Finally Gamic began to circle them, slowly at first then slightly faster. Each time he swept around it seemed to Katook that the circle was getting smaller. And for those brief moments all of Bo-hibba felt as one again and filled with hope.

Katook stole another look. He saw Gamic running, his head thrown back, his eyes staring up at the dark, cloudy sky, his tail whipping wildly from side to side. Katook quickly clenched his eyes shut. Then suddenly the temple gates slammed shut and all was still.

No one moved for a long time. At last Katook heard the rustle of his father's fur as he stood up and arched his back. Katook and the others opened their eyes, hoping the ceremony had revealed a vast carpet of bright stars to foretell a day of sunshine. But there were no stars. No moon. Only the cold blanket of gray clouds.

"Come," Hano whispered. "Let's go home. All is done that can be done. May Fossah forgive us."

"For what?" asked Katook. "What have we done wrong?"

"Only the Fossah knows," answered Hano wearily. "But now, with the Fossah's blessing, it will be revealed to Gamic so that he can tell us how to make amends."

Katook wiped the mud from his knees. He had never heard his father sound so tired and empty. Katook wished there were some way he could comfort him. Hano, like everyone else in Bo-hibba, had hoped this ceremony—the Ancient of Ancients—would clear the skies and bring back the sun. But they had failed.

Chapter Two
THE DARE

The wind lashed the villagers with icy gusts as they left and headed home. Katook didn't mind. *At least this way I can be outside a little longer before I'm trapped at home for who knows how long*, he thought. Up ahead he spotted a beautiful, creamy striped tail. The tail belonged to Adara.

Ever since Katook was a young kit, he'd thought Adara was the most beautiful lemur in all of Kattakuk. Unfortunately, so did his best friend, Naxo, who was up ahead on the path. Katook watched him weave in and out of the line toward Adara. Katook broke into a lope, and just as Naxo slid up to one side of her, he slid up to the other.

Katook whispered, "Hi, Adara. I saw your tail. It's really clean."

Adara acknowledged the clumsy compliment with a sidelong glance and the faintest hint of a smile, but continued walking.

Not to be outdone by his friend, Naxo whispered in her other ear,

"The cleanest and fluffiest tail probably in all of Bo-hibba."

Adara gave Naxo a brief, sweet smile, then looked to Katook as if waiting for him to come up with an even finer compliment.

While Katook struggled to think of something brilliant to say, Naxo pulled Adara off to the side of the path. Katook hurried after them. Once they were out of earshot of the others, Naxo said, "I know where the Indriis carry the offerings. I know the hidden place where the priests serve the Great One."

Adara stared at Naxo. "I don't believe you. Only the priests and the Indriis know where that place is!"

"And now I do, too," Naxo insisted.

"Well, even if you do, it's forbidden for any but the priests to speak of it."

"You're just talking," Katook said quickly. "You're making it all up."

"I've never seen it, but I know where it is," Naxo bragged. "It's right there." He pointed past the cliffs, down toward the Forbidden Trees. "I've never been there, because—"

"Because it's forbidden!" repeated Adara.

Naxo had her full attention now, and he was smiling broadly. "I'm not afraid of those old priests. And the Indriis are fierce but they're slow. Katook's the one who's scared, not me. Aren't you, Katook? You'd rather stay on this nice, safe path like a scared little kit on his first day of tree climbing."

"Don't listen to him, Katook," Adara urged. But it was too late. It had become a contest of wills, and neither Katook nor Naxo was going to back down.

"I'm not afraid if you're not," said Katook, meeting Naxo's challenge.

"You're sure?" Naxo taunted him.

"Of course I'm sure," said Katook, though he could feel his heart pounding.

Naxo looked down into the dark, forbidden place. "We'll see about that." He cut a glance at Adara.

"Naxo, don't—" she began.

Laughing, Naxo took a short running start—and jumped off the cliff!

"Naxo!" Katook called out. He and Adara rushed to the edge of the path in time to see Naxo plunge through the dark canopy of trees and out of sight.

Without a pause Katook jumped after his friend. Falling through the air, he was only dimly aware of Adara's voice calling after him. He crashed through the whiplike upper branches of an old fig tree and fell into pitch darkness. He felt leaves slapping his face and branches hitting him in the ribs.

Finally he landed with a great thud on the muddy loam of the jungle floor.

"Ooof," he said. Gingerly, he sat up.

"Katook, is that you?" he heard Naxo whisper from somewhere in the dark.

"Yes," Katook whispered back. "Where are you?"

"Follow me." Then Katook heard his friend's paw-falls moving away from him. He loped slowly toward the sound, hoping he wouldn't plow headlong into a tree.

For a time the only sounds were their paws hitting the soft ground and their wildly beating hearts. The two young lemurs ran deeper and deeper into the forbidden jungle until, mysteriously, the darkness fell away and was replaced by a pale blue haze.

They stopped running and stared at each other's feet. They were glowing brightly with an unnatural bluish light.

Then Katook noticed the mushrooms. They were everywhere, and the ones they had stepped on were now emitting a sky-blue phosphorescence.

"Where are we?" Katook whispered. "You have no idea, do you?"

Naxo's eyes were wide with fear.

"Naxo, it's okay, we'll find our way home."

"Maybe this was a bad idea," Naxo admitted in a small voice.

"Look! Over there!" Katook pointed toward a glow of torchlight flickering through the trees. "Follow me!"

They moved quietly through the thick foliage, heading straight for the torches. Suddenly Katook stopped, rose up on his hind legs, and cocked his head to the side. Then he ducked back down.

"What is it?" asked Naxo.

"Shhh, up there."

Less than two tree-lengths away, Gamic was leading the other masked priests down ancient stone stairs carved into the side of the cliff. Behind them came Reet, carrying the wicker offering basket on his wide shoulders, and the other Indriis.

"I'll bet there's a secret passageway from under the temple," whispered Katook.

"I told you this is where they come," Naxo said, sounding a little braver.

Katook and Naxo hid behind the great, wide leaves of a giant black orchid. Then, as if drawn against his will, Katook started crawling after the priests.

"Katook!" Naxo whispered harshly. "Don't—"

"Come on," Katook whispered over his shoulder. "But be careful not to touch the mushrooms. They'll give us away."

Why didn't they run away? Why they didn't race up the secret stairway and find their way home before they were found out? There are two answers. One is simple, the other isn't. The simple answer is that they were young and, in all young lemurs, curiosity is a powerful thing. The other answer is that they followed Gamic because that was how it was meant to be.

Katook and Naxo slipped between fleshy leaves and under heavy vines, always careful to stay clear of the light-emitting mushrooms. They moved farther and farther into the rain forest, past red, oily-looking lizards, snakes with lemon-yellow bands, and spiders as clear as glass.

Gamic and his troop finally stopped at a jagged fence made entirely of bones, moon-white and brittle with age. In a clearing just beyond the bone fence was the great Fossah!

Terrified, Katook and Naxo pressed their bodies into the moist soil. Naxo said quietly, "I'm looking but I don't understand."

Katook slowly realized what he was seeing. It was a colossal statue, crafted out of wicker and polished with amber beeswax. Gamic and the others stepped through a gap in the bone fence and slowly approached the statue. In silence, he gestured to Reet. The Indrii guard set the basket on a stone pedestal in the great claws of the sculpted Fossah.

Then the priests formed a circle around the Fossah. The guards formed a circle around the priests, facing outward, their eyes fixed on the dark jungle.

"Look, even the guards know better than to gaze upon the forbidden," whispered Naxo. "What are we doing here?" He crawled after Katook through the gap in the fence.

"Shhh," Katook whispered. "If you want to go, go. But I'm staying."

Katook turned his attention away from Naxo just in time to see Gamic circle the offering basket in a slow, rhythmic dance. The High Priest took one of the figs meant for the Fossah, and raised it up toward the blessed statue. Then he did the unimaginable.

He lifted his mask and ate the fig.

Katook couldn't believe what he had seen. Gamic took

out another fig and ate that one, too. The other priests joined him, noisily gorging themselves on the sacred fruit.

"Naxo, do you see this?" whispered Katook, incredulously.

Naxo answered in barely a whisper, "Yes, but I don't believe it."

"While our families starve, Gamic and his priests eat not only what little we have left, but what is meant for the Fossah, too!"

Katook and Naxo watched as the priests betrayed the sacred rites and all the lemurs of Bo-hibba. For the first time, Katook understood why Gamic and the other priests weren't as thin and ragged as everyone else. He knew that this was terribly wrong . . . but who could he ever tell? He and Naxo never should have witnessed this.

Katook heard it before he saw it—a *swish*, then a solid *thwack*. Then saw Naxo's tail nervously, unconsciously flick against the bone fence. Katook quickly grabbed his friend's tail, but not before Reet swung his gaze in their direction.

Terrified, Naxo took a tiny step backward and landed squarely on a giant mushroom, which exploded in a cloud of bright blue light.

Enraged, the temple guard pointed straight at Katook and Naxo.

Naxo tumbled backward, and the bone fence crashed around him with the sound of a hundred bolts of lightning striking at once.

Katook quickly burrowed under the pile of broken bones and whispered, "Stay down!"

But it was too late. Naxo took off in a blind panic as fast as he could, hammering mushrooms as he ran, leaving a brightly lit path of blue in his wake. The Indriis chased after the young kit, their torches held high.

With mushrooms exploding under his feet, Naxo sprinted madly through the jungle, dizzy with terror. A mound of dense underbrush rose up straight ahead of him.

The Indriis ran harder. Reet, the strongest of them all, was closest to Naxo. He leapt, his claws extended. Naxo screamed and vanished into the thick undergrowth.

"*Naxo!*" Katook called out.

Reet spun around, pointed at Katook, and screamed, "There's another one! Get him!"

Katook bolted to his feet—then suddenly the flames in every torch blew out and the pale blue mushroom light vanished. Everything was black and still. And out of this stillness came a sound from the deep heart of the jungle, from the soul of the land.

The gathering sound made every living creature press his body into the earth—the guards, even the priests, even Gamic himself, fell prostrate, their eyes hidden beneath their paws. All but Katook, who was so filled with awe and dread that he could not move, could barely breathe.

Perhaps he was simply too young to know what was happening, but in that moment Katook, a simple lemur from Kattakuk, was the only one standing in front of all that is Sun and Star and Day and Moon and Night. He felt a presence move toward him out of the darkness. Then, in the moment before he clenched his eyes, he saw something magnificent and terrible staring down at him from a great height beyond the trees, beyond the sky, beyond the Beyond. The Fossah.

19

How long he stood there is not known or told, but at length Katook realized the presence was gone. The forest around him was filled with a hollow silence, like a great hunger. The priests appeared unconscious, their arms splayed at their sides. And the Indriis lay frozen where they had dropped, their eyes sealed shut.

Katook called out in a small, frightened voice, "Naxo, can you hear me?"

Only silence answered him.

Katook didn't know how long the guards would sleep, but he knew that he had to get out of this place. He wanted to make his way back to the stairway carved into the hillside and hurry home. But he couldn't leave his friend. He slowly moved toward the spot where Naxo had disappeared, hoping that the Indriis would remain asleep.

Katook walked lightly, his paws barely touching the ground. Then he heard faint murmurings as the Indriis began to waken. He felt a surge of panic grip his heart.

Hide, quickly! Anywhere! his mind screamed blindly. But to go forward meant stepping over them, and to retreat meant running back toward the huge statue of the Fossah and the priests. To his left were more Indriis, and to his right were the cliffs.

The cliffs! Katook sprinted across the forest floor to the cliff face. It was mossy and slick with leafy plants, and he struggled to gain a hold. Pausing to catch his breath, he felt a draft of cold, moist air on his muzzle. Leaning into the wall, he found a very narrow cleft—a cave hidden behind a curtain of vines.

"Quickly!" screamed Reet as the Indriis climbed after Katook.

Katook smelled their acrid sweat. He wriggled through vines and squeezed into the narrow opening. He could hear the Indriis trying to claw their way after him, but the cave's mouth was far too small for their massive bodies.

It was pitch black. He felt solid stone under his feet—damp, cold, and perfectly flat. He took another tiny step, and the floor dropped out beneath him. He slid down a narrow chute of cold, smooth stone. Eventually the tunnel leveled out, and he came to a gentle stop.

Katook sat still, his heart racing. "Hello?" he called out, but heard only a very faint echo in return. Katook pressed his ear to the tunnel's floor, and heard a distant roaring sound from someplace far ahead. He began to crawl.

As he made his way toward the sound, the mysterious roaring grew until it filled the entire tunnel. At last Katook could crawl no more. Tired and miserable, he curled into a ball and let sleep claim him.

Katook woke chilled and lonely. There was nothing else to do but crawl again. He rounded a sharp corner and blinked. He was bathed in a shimmering, brilliant pale aqua light. Just ahead of him was a wall that was not a wall, but a sheet of glowing, cascading water. Blue light was shining through it. He was on the inside of a waterfall.

Katook leapt backward, slamming hard into rock. Like all lemurs, he was deathly afraid of water. Shuddering with fear, he searched for an escape, but as he did he noticed a rough drawing carved into the wall behind him.

He looked more closely. It was an image of the great Fossah. Its eyes were painted sapphire blue—a color Katook had never seen in eyes. Even stranger, the image seemed to stare back at him with a gaze both peaceful and comforting. It looked nothing at all like the frightening wicker statue. It didn't feel anything like the powerful, mysterious being that had loomed over him in the Forbidden Trees. *Could this be the same Fossah?* Katook wondered.

Katook closed his own eyes and pressed his forehead against the image and as he did, a great calm spread through him, as though he were lying in his mother's embrace, safe and warm. He stared at the wall of water again. Just beyond the aqua sheet, Katook saw the blurry, hazy shapes of trees.

He took another step toward the edge where rock ended and nothing began. He felt strangely compelled to leap through the water. He simply had to know what it would feel like. Cold water sprayed his face. He wiped it from his fur with a tentative paw. And while every instinct in him screamed *No!*—he closed his eyes, wrapped his tail around his body, spread his arms wide, and jumped.

Chapter Three
THE PRICE

He fell through a freezing mist as heavy as rain. And then he landed with a hard splash on an enormous lily pad. He bounced twice and tumbled face-first into gooey mud at the edge of an ice-cold river.

"Get up!" a voice commanded. A black-clawed foot kicked Katook in the ribs.

Dripping wet, his fur tangled with muddy leaves, Katook rolled onto his back and stared up into Reet's cruel eyes.

"Naxo . . . ," started Katook. "Have you seen—"

"Bind him!"

Katook stammered, "B-but I just want to know if Naxo's all right."

Reet yanked Katook to his feet then threw him to the ground in front of his underlings. "And gag him, too!"

Two Indrii guards stuffed a braided vine into Katook's mouth and tied it behind his head. The vine was coarse and tasted sour. They lashed his wrists in front of him. Reet moved close to Katook, and Katook could hear him sniffing. He knew that Reet was inhaling the smell of his fear.

Reet whispered, "One word about what you saw in the Forbidden Trees and I swear to you, it will be your last word."

Katook stared straight ahead, afraid to meet Reet's ruthless gaze.

Reet gave the end of the vine a hard tug. Katook stumbled then caught his balance as Reet started dragging him back toward Kattakuk.

The northernmost boundary of the village was marked by a huge boulder. Reet climbed on top of the marker, arched his powerful back, and bellowed their approach.

By the time Katook and his guards arrived in Kattakuk, all the lemurs were gathered in the center of the village. Bound and gagged, Katook searched the crowd for his family. He found his parents flanked by a pair of Indrii guards. Oola was sobbing, tears streaking her cheeks. His father looked weak with fear.

Katook wanted to run to them. To feel his mother's arms around him. To hear his father tell him that everything would be all right. But Reet held Katook firmly by the scruff of his neck and hissed, "If you tell them what you saw in the Forbidden Trees, you and your family will all die. Spare them or have them killed. It's up to you."

Oola took a step toward him, but a guard held her back.

Katook's eyes darted helplessly around the crowd. That's when he saw Naxo. But his friend quickly looked away and hid himself in the crowd.

At first Katook was relieved to see his best friend alive and safe. Then he felt a surge of anger. Clearly, Naxo had not admitted that it was it was his idea, not Katook's, to enter the Forbidden Trees.

The anger passed quickly. *He's as scared as I am*, Katook realized. *Of course he didn't say anything.*

Reet dragged Katook onto the path to the temple. It was lined on either side by Indrii guards. He leaned

walk slow and enjoy the stroll. This will be your last time through the village."

A huge explosion shuddered the ground, setting off a plume of blue sparks. All the lemurs dropped to their knees. Even the fierce Indriis knelt under the sparkling blue rain. All but Reet, who kept marching Katook forward toward the temple.

There Gamic, the High Priest, sat on a charred fig stump. He wore the black Robes of Passing and an ebony mask, and carried a burning staff in his paw. He silenced the crowd with two thunderous *thuds* of his staff.

"Bring him," Gamic instructed.

Katook's whole body trembled. Katook felt Reet's huge paws on his neck forcing him to his knees.

"Without the return of the sun and the rains, all the lemurs of Bo-hibba will starve," the High Priest began. "We pray to the Fossah night and day, yet the Fossah remains displeased. Now we know why. Finally we can clearly see the wicked one who has drawn the Fossah's wrath!"

Is that me? Katook wondered. *Is the Long Winter my fault?* But that couldn't be right. Katook knew he'd seen what he shouldn't have seen. Still, the Long Winter had started long before that.

"Stand, Katook, son of Hano and Oola, brother of Kai and Lina!" Gamic bellowed. "Stand and prepare to receive your just fate!"

Katook trembled. The priest's paw flashed out, sharp nails extended, slashing at the vines that bound his wrists. With his paws free, Katook wiped the leaves and mud from his face and turned to look for his parents. It was then that he heard the villagers gasp.

"His eyes!" yelled one of the guards. "Look at his eyes!"

"Turn and face me!" Gamic roared at Katook.

But when he looked directly at the High Priest, Katook saw Gamic flinch; saw his eyes widen with shock.

"Free his mouth to speak," Gamic ordered, and the priests removed Katook's gag.

"What is it?" asked Katook, frightened. "What's wrong with my eyes?"

"You've been cursed," answered Gamic in a throaty whisper.

"I don't understand." Then Katook saw his face reflected on the polished ebony surface of the High Priest's mask.

He couldn't believe what he was seeing. His eyes were no longer amber, like those of every other lemur in Kattakuk. His eyes were now a deep, sapphire blue.

Gamic pointed at Katook and cried, "Look! He has enraged the Great One, and the Fossah has marked him for his insolence!" Then the High Priest lifted his blazing staff and held it over Katook. "He is no longer *of* us. He is a traitor to his people and must be banished from his land!"

They all knew that Gamic spoke for the great Fossah, the protector of all of Bo-hibba. Gamic's power was so great that even Katook's parents remained silent.

"From this moment forward," the High Priest proclaimed,
"Katook of Kattakuk, son of Hano and Oola, is no more.
He has no home. He has no people. He will walk alone forever."

Katook's mother let out a wail. She was sobbing. His sister met
his blue gaze and then looked quickly away, tears bright on her face.
Even his father, who held Kai tight to his chest, could not meet
Katook's eyes. He had only one son left now.

Katook wanted to scream at Gamic and the other priests:
You are the criminals, not me!

Gamic leaned close and whispered quietly, so only Katook could hear, "Stay silent, young Katook, or I will have your parents killed here and now."

Katook had never been outside Kattakuk. Never been away from his family. He could not imagine the loneliness. His heart felt as if it would explode.

That's when he saw the cage. Reet and another Indrii brought it forward and set it on the ground in front of Katook. It was sturdy, made of dry, thickly woven twigs. It was the most frightening thing Katook had ever seen.

"Get in," ordered Reet.

Katook stood frozen with terror.

Reet threw him into the cage and secured its door with strong, green vines.

Inside, Katook couldn't stand, could barely move his arms. He peered through a tiny gap in the twig wall and saw Gamic face the village as he sang Bo-hibba's banishment song.

> Banished, outcast, vagabond,
> Never shall we look upon
> He that we have driven out.
> Far away you will stay
> Out . . . out . . . out!

Out! Out! Katook's heart broke at the thought that he would never again see his home.

Suddenly Katook felt the cage being hoisted into the air, then slammed down hard on something solid. He bit his tongue and tasted blood in his mouth. The horrible stench of a moa—the huge flightless birds trained by the temple guards—made Katook gag. Reet lashed the basket to the back of one of these enormous creatures.

Katook felt dizzy with panic. He struggled for air. Reet leaned close to the cage and said in a vicious whisper, "If you ever return, Blue Eyes, I will kill you."

Then Reet led the moa away from Kattakuk and toward the distant gap in the mountains that was the home of the sleeping sun. The last thing Katook heard before he passed out was a loud whack as Reet slapped the moa's rump, sending it on its way.

31

They traveled for two days.

On the second day Katook caught glimpses of brown grass, dirt, rocks, and gravel. Then he heard biting and scratching, and suddenly he felt the basket moving. It slid off the moa's back and crashed to the ground with a bone-jarring *thud*.

"Hello . . . ," said Katook, but only silence answered him.

He saw the moa slowly walking away from him.

"Please, before you go, at least let me out!" begged Katook.

The moa took a few more steps, then turned around. It gazed down at Katook with bright, curious eyes.

"I won't follow you back," said Katook. "I promise."

The moa paused, then bit through the vines that secured the cage.

"Thank you!" Katook said as he pushed open the cage door.

Katook stepped out and stretched his cramped muscles. He heard a strange roaring, which grew louder, then quieter, then louder again. The ground around him was stark white. And beyond the white, a vast expanse of blue that seemed to go on forever. *It looks like water,* Katook thought. *But how can that be? There's so much of it!*

"Where am I?" Katook said in a small, frightened voice. "And where will I go from here?"

33

Chapter Four
THE BEYOND

Katook was lost and utterly miserable. He had a dull ache in his heart. He missed his family. He missed his home. He sat down on the sand and felt its wet coldness through his fur. Pangs of hunger rumbled through him. He wanted desperately to run back to Kattakuk, but he knew he was unwelcome there. No, worse. He would be killed if he returned. So he just sat there on the cold sand, numb with confusion and paralyzed with grief.

The wide beach was bordered on one side by a turquoise ocean and on the other by a carpet of purple-flowered ice plants, their spiky, succulent leaves sharp green against patches of white sand. Rising here and there from this blanket of dark green and purple were the rough, round trunks of palm trees.

Katook's eyes followed one of these unfamiliar trees higher and higher, to the very top, where he saw a silly-looking tuft of dry green leaves that hissed quietly in the breeze. The tree had no crooks for climbing, no branches to lie on.

What kind of worthless tree is that? And what kind of worthless place is this? Katook wondered, feeling quite sorry for himself.

He closed his eyes, wanting to lose himself in thoughts of home, but all he could think about was the hunger in his belly. He was starving. He opened his eyes. He knew that if he didn't find something to eat soon, he might fall asleep and never wake.

A dark, shriveled piece of seaweed lay next to him. It didn't look appetizing, but it did look edible. Katook decided that a stomach as empty as his couldn't afford to be choosy. Tentatively he reached for the shrively piece of seaweed, but the instant his paw touched it, it moved!

Katook jumped. "What's this?" he said out loud. Never before

had he tried to eat anything that moved, except of course a piece of fruit that might sway in a breeze. But this was not in a tree and there was no breeze.

Katook decided it must be alive. He crept toward the seaweed and crouched low, so as not to frighten it.

"Hello," he whispered, feeling a little silly talking to a plant.

The seaweed was silent. Katook waited. He slowly reached out and just as he was about to touch it again, it began to slowly slither toward the water.

"Wait," he commanded. "Don't leave!"

The seaweed ignored Katook and continued its journey toward the sea. On all fours, Katook followed behind. It occurred to him that, of course, the seaweed wasn't listening. It didn't appear to have ears to hear him with—or a mouth to reply. Katook felt more ridiculous than ever.

Frustrated, Katook glanced around for something less mobile to eat. He was just about to walk away when the seaweed rolled onto one side, and out from under it came a small head. The head was gray, with two large blinking eyes and a beaky mouth. The animal's body seemed to be covered with an oblong shell. Two leathery little legs stuck out on either side of the shell. They started frantically fanning the sand, inching forward. Katook watched, amazed, as the baby sea turtle started down the beach, racing for the ocean as fast as it could go.

"Wait!" cried Katook. "Please stay and talk with me."

"No time. No time," said the baby turtle without even turning its crinkly neck to look back at Katook. "Must go. Must go."

"But why?" Katook asked. "What's the hurry?"

The answer swooped from the sky with a loud squawk and a dark flash of beak. It was a giant frigate bird, and it was determined to catch the baby turtle before it reached the safety of the ocean. With talons extended, the bird swooped toward the baby turtle. At the last instant, the frightened hatchling changed direction. Sand exploded next to the turtle as the bird's talons raked the ground, just missing it. With a frustrated squawk, the frigate bird climbed into the sky to gather speed for another strike.

Just then Katook heard another voice, almost identical to the first. "Run for your lives! Must hurry. Must go. No time to say hello."

Katook looked and saw, all around him, tiny rough gray heads and the newborn blinking eyes of tens of frightened baby turtles, all digging themselves out from under the sand, each of them on a mad dash—as much as turtles can dash—toward the ocean.

Overhead, the sky darkened with the beating wings of a flock of frigate birds. They were flying so close together that their wings

almost touched. The mass of angry black birds circled faster and faster, until one by one they dived down on the helpless turtles.

"No! Stop it!" Katook cried as one of the birds snatched a baby turtle only inches from the safety of the water. Katook's eyes widened with horror as the bird flew high into the sky then released the turtle. The poor turtle's little arms flailed helplessly in the air; then it smashed onto a field of rock, and the frigate bird lazily floated down to eat it.

Another frigate bird swooped down. And another.

"Leave them alone!" Katook shouted.

Unable to bear this one-sided attack any longer, Katook grabbed a sturdy piece of driftwood. He began running up and down the beach, waving his stick, trying to frighten off the diving frigate birds while, at the same time, being careful not to step on the tiny creatures streaming toward the ocean.

He screamed at the birds until his voice grew hoarse. His legs and arms burned with fatigue, but the sweet sight of the baby turtles, their

dull, pebble-gray shells turning shiny and bright as they slipped into the safety of the ocean, kept him going.

Katook ran back and forth across the beach until the last of the sea turtles was in the water. Exhausted, his stomach churning with hunger, arms aching from waving the stick, Katook collapsed on the sand. He lay there for a long time, so still you might have thought him dead. The sun pushed through the clouds and shone hot and full on his face. He could feel his nose beginning to burn in the sun, but he was too tired to move. Too tired even to crawl to a nearby palm tree's beckoning shade. He closed his eyes and fell into a deep sleep.

The sun had fallen halfway across the sky when a spray of water woke Katook from his dreams of home. The water felt fresh and cold on his face. Some of it dribbled onto his mouth. He licked his lips and was surprised that the water tasted salty, like tears. Then he heard a deep and rumbling voice. "I owe you so much, brave one. How can I repay you?"

Katook rolled onto his side and saw two huge eyes, as large as his paws, blinking at him from the head of a huge sea turtle.

"Repay me? For what?" asked Katook as he slowly got to his feet.

"For giving me my babies," replied the sea turtle. "They swam to me and told me how you saved their lives. How bold and fierce you were in fighting the darkness from the sky. So please, tell me what I can do to repay you for your bravery."

"You don't owe me anything," replied Katook. "Anyone would have done the same."

"But no one did and no one ever has before. Now, don't be difficult, furry one, and listen to me. I've seen gold shimmering on the ocean's floor. I can carry a great deal of it on my back. Stay here and I will bring you some."

"Thank you, but I have no need for gold."

"Then I've seen pools of molten stone glowing and sizzling at the water's edge. I will place some of them in a large, very thick shell and carry it back for you. Then you will possess it and hold its power."

"Thank you," Katook said politely, "I have no need for power, either."

"What a strange little being you are," the mother sea turtle murmured. "Surely there must be something you want."

"Well, actually, there is one thing," Katook said very softly.

"Anything," replied the mother sea turtle.

"I can't go back home again," said Katook sheepishly. "So I'd really like to find others like me so I won't feel so alone."

"Like you?" repeated the mother sea turtle.

"Others who look like me," explained Katook. "Other lemurs."

The mother sea turtle studied Katook a moment, then nodded. "Of course," she said. "I'll take you to them."

"Oh, I don't want to trouble you," Katook said quickly. "If you'll just point in the right direction, I'm sure I can find them myself."

The sea turtle cocked her leathery head and pointed with her beak. "That way. Across the wide blue to the first shore beyond the horizon."

Katook stared out at the water.

"You're afraid of the wide blue, aren't you?" asked the mother sea turtle.

"More than anything," Katook replied.

"Anything? Are you more afraid of it than of being alone?"

Katook fell silent.

"Climb onto my back," urged the mother sea turtle. "Your longing will devour your fear, I promise."

Katook hesitated, but he knew he couldn't bear being so alone. He scrambled up onto the sea turtle's slippery shell and held fast to the thick rim just behind her head. Scrunching his eyes closed, Katook felt the turtle's front flippers make two great pulls in the sand, and then he seemed to be gliding. He imagined it would feel like this to fly.

Although he kept his eyes tightly closed, he knew that they were in the water and moving farther from the shore with each stroke of the turtle's legs.

Moments passed that seemed like hours.

"Are we there yet?" asked Katook, his eyes clenched and his paws clutching tightly to the turtle's shell.

"No, but we're not far away."

"How much longer?"

"That's hard to say. It depends on the tides. We should be there in a pair of dippings of the sun and of the moon."

"What?" exclaimed Katook, opening his eyes for the first time. "Two entire days! But you said we weren't far away. I thought we were almost there!"

"We *are* almost there," replied the sea turtle. "On many journeys I have watched the sun and moon dip into the wide blue more times than I can count. This won't take but one of each."

Two days! Katook thought. The reality of his situation hit him like a club. He was in the middle of the ocean, with no end in sight, hungry and lonely. Suddenly Katook sensed that they were gaining speed. He shut his eyes again and tightened his grip on the turtle's shell.

"There . . . do you feel that?" she asked.

"I feel something," said Katook uncertainly. "We're going faster, aren't we?"

"It's the wide blue, not me. She's taken us in. Her currents and my legs will swim together now. She must like you. She must want you to find your kind."

Curious, Katook managed to crack his eyes open. He looked back toward the shore and was amazed by how far they had traveled in such a short time. What only minutes ago had been a wide band of beach was now a dark line on the horizon.

Katook and the sea turtle traveled like that all day—until the land was only a memory. Katook no longer shut his eyes but stared out at the ocean, wide and empty. He realized his fear had faded and his breathing was almost normal again.

"You must get lonely out here all by yourself," Katook called out over the sound of the sea rushing past them.

"Lonely? We're far from alone. Look down, furry one."

For the first time, Katook looked past the sea turtle's shell and saw creatures of all different sizes and colors and shapes swimming directly under them; he realized that he was riding on the surface of a giant party. Through the clear blue water he could see a pink cloud of tiny shrimp moving together as if of one mind. Dashing back and forth through this cloud were ginger pearlfish and opal allotoca, all of them keeping an eye on a fierce green-and-yellow dunkleoseus. The powerful sharklike predator lunged at a rough-backed monk seal, who made playful circles around him, carefully staying just out of reach. Dolphins pirouetted in lightning arcs. But most breathtaking of all were

the great serpentine whales as they breached the surface and spouted.

"Have they been with us all this time?" Katook asked.

"Some have," the mother sea turtle answered. "Some have come and gone. More will arrive soon. As I said, we are far from alone."

Later that night, after the sun had doused her fire in the ocean and the sky was black with night, the mother sea turtle paused to rest. Katook knew that she was letting the ocean's current do the work for her while she slept.

Katook lay on his stomach, stretched across the turtle's wide back, and gazed down into the moonlit water at steamy-blue luminescent jellyfish and tiny, darting lemon-yellow angelfish. Then he rolled onto his back and watched the shimmering flashes of flying fish, their wet-sleek bodies leaping over him then disappearing into the star-sprinkled black water. Comforted by the ocean's gentle rocking, he watched the stars swirl overhead until their brightness dimmed, and he fell asleep.

Katook dreamed of being an explorer on his way to visit places he could barely imagine. "A sky-eyed explorer," he heard himself say in his dream. He liked the way it sounded and liked the way it felt even more.

He slept late into the morning. He slept on even as they neared land and the air grew chilled and seagulls squawked overheard and pelicans dropped from the sky, beak-first, into the water with loud splashes. He slept even as the sea turtle caught a wave and rode it

42

toward shore, the blue crest of the wave falling gently over Katook in a watery tube.

Not wanting to wake Katook, the mother sea turtle carefully negotiated the surf and gently eased her clumsy body from the white water. She carried him to the water's edge and, being careful not to wake him, rolled the young lemur off her back and left him there on the sand, just beyond the warm ebb and flow of the tide.

"Sky-eyed explorer," the mother sea turtle said to herself with a smile. As she turned back to the ocean, she noticed that Katook's tail was curled on the sand in the shape of a perfect question mark. "So many questions to ask," she muttered to herself as she slipped back into the water. "So many answers to find, " she said as she swam away.

Chapter Five
ACCO

When Katook finally woke up, the first thing he saw was a gaping mouth, filled with razor-sharp teeth, only inches from his face! He leapt backward, terrified.

Crouching low, he stared at the giant-jawed creature. It had a long silver-gray body without arms and a wide, flat tail that shifted lazily from side to side in the surf. Katook slowly circled the creature, his fur raised. And though its mouth remained open in a silent snarl and its tail continued its slow, menacing movement, its eyes never moved.

"Hello?" Katook asked nervously, ready to sprint away at the slightest threat. "I'm over here."

The creature's unblinking eyes stared straight ahead, as if it were ignoring him.

"Can't you hear me?" said Katook, irritated with the creature for being so rude. "Look, I'm right here!"

But it refused to turn and face him.

Curious, Katook picked up a pebble and tossed it gently at the sea creature. The stone bounced off its silver hide without rousing a flicker of a reaction. Katook inched closer, grabbed a stick, and gingerly poked the beast. Still it refused to turn its giant head in his direction.

His fear ebbing, Katook faced the creature. Looking into its glossy eyes, he saw that the life had left the sea beast. The only reason its tail swayed from side to side was because it was floating on the tide.

Katook sat back on his haunches, lonelier than ever. This shore looked nothing like the one on Bo-hibba. Great sandstone rocks jutted up from the waves. A narrow, rocky beach ended in the shadow of a steep headland. A few trees—twisted and stunted—clung to the top of the rock face. A cloud of seabirds whirled overhead, their harsh cries filling the air.

A few of the birds started to spiral down toward the dead monster. Remembering the frigate birds, Katook backed away and gazed at the cliffs. His nostrils quivered. A smoky, musky odor was floating on the breeze. No, it was many odors—a tangle of animals and foods and other things, all of them strange and exotic. The scents seemed to be coming from up on top of the cliff.

Seeing a narrow path that wove to the top of the headland, Katook began to follow it. In time he came to a high wall that was crudely made of dried mud, seaweed, and sun-bleached timbers. Katook gazed up, taking in the smell of food and the sounds of countless creatures coming from someplace behind that wall. Curious and very hungry, he climbed to the top of the wall—then paused, stunned at the sight before him.

Spread out in front of Katook was a riot of brilliantly colored fabric and oddly shaped wooden structures. Even from high up on the wall it was almost impossible to see down into the maze of streets that made up the town because the entire place was shaded by a patchwork of roofs. Crowds of strange creatures passed busily to and fro. Katook saw that some were predator-folk and others prey-folk. Yet they all hurried along, barely seeming to notice each other unless they stopped to barter. In the distance, at the northwestern edge of the town, where the seashore turned inward, there was a harbor filled with bobbing boats, their colored sails rustling in a light breeze. To the east, yellow grassy fields vanished into the mistier green of the horizon.

Katook took a deep breath and sprang from the wall. In ten bounds or so he was lost in the crowd and swept along into the town. He soon found himself standing in the middle of a bustling marketplace.

All around him, everyone seemed busy buying or selling things. There were strange fruits and vegetables, and playthings and trinkets and sparkling things that the animals here wore. There were tools and utensils, and cauldrons and vessels of all kinds. The wares were arranged on tables and benches, overflowing from giant gourds, stacked on the ground, and hanging from beams in baskets and woven nets.

The place was packed with animals of all shapes and sizes, bristly animals with short muscled legs and sleek ones with long elegant legs. Katook saw creatures that moved very slowly, and those that hopped, and still others who ran from place to place, as if in a terrible hurry.

Surely this is the place to find others like me, he thought.

He scanned the crowd, searching for the familiarity of a ringed tail like his, or a white chest with gray arms and legs, or best of all, golden lemur eyes that would look back at him and make him feel not so alone. But in the middle of the bustle and hustle, with all those animals, Katook couldn't see anyone who looked even a *little* bit like him.

Katook reached a crowd of animals who were gathered around a troupe of acrobats. The acrobats were performing for a giant ground sloth who sat regally on a platform, looking very large and important. A koala did a handstand on the paws of a kangaroo. Two gibbons spun through the air in spectacular double flips, landed lightly, and bowed to the giant sloth.

The crowd broke out in enthusiastic applause. Everyone, that is, except for Katook, who, though impressed with the acrobats, was feeling horribly distracted by the ache of hunger and the smell of sweet fruit on the breeze. The smell was so delicious that Katook's churning stomach growled even louder. The rumbling in his belly was so loud that when the acrobat called out to the giant sloth, "Are you pleased, Mr. Mayor?" all Katook heard was: ". . . You peas or . . ."

Katook turned to an armadillo and asked, "His peas or what?"

46

The armadillo stared strangely at Katook, then turned his attention back toward the acrobats. Katook moved toward the scent. As he caught another yummy waft of sweet fruit, he closed his eyes and inhaled deeply.

"You look quite hungry, long-fingered one," said a deep voice quite close to Katook's ear.

Katook turned to see a bristly-maned, spindly-legged cud-chewer standing next to him. And sitting on its back was a plump, squinty-eyed spiny anteater, who chimed in, "Quite hungry indeed. A shame for one as athletic as you appear to be." The anteater bowed slightly and continued, "Fleng I am and Plod is he. Horned and prickly, we two be. I am an anteater. Plod is a gnu. And you?"

"I'm a lemur. And it's very nice to meet you."

"I'm sure the pleasure is all ours, is it not, Fleng?" said the cud-chewer.

"Ours, yes. Or soon shall be, if I am not mistaken, you friend of me," said the anteater, who apparently insisted on rhyming everything he said, no matter how horrible or forced the rhyme. "But it's clear you are hungry and have traveled far. Please allow us to nourish you with something here at this bar."

And with that Fleng flung a shiny bead to the merchant. Quick as can be, a banana appeared, peeled and ready, creamy and sweet, held in Fleng's fat little paw in front of Katook's quivering nose.

"Please, be our guest," prompted Plod.

Not wanting to be rude and eat alone, Katook hesitated.

"Perhaps you'd rather something less sweet?" asked Plod.

"Oh, no," Katook cried out. "It looks perfect."

Fleng handed Katook the banana. "Nibble or bite, however you like."

Katook took the banana and chomped off a piece ravenously. It was delicious. In fact, it *was* perfect. He wondered if this was because he so hungry, or because it was the gift of a stranger, and as his mother once told him, kindness can awaken the senses in the most mysterious ways. Whatever the reason, Katook had never enjoyed a banana as much as this one, and he was certain of one thing—he wanted another.

"If you think that was fine," said Fleng as he hopped back on Plod's back, "taste our honey-dipped fruits. They are simply divine."

"H-honey-dipped?" Katook stammered, his mouth watering at the thought.

"They're quite nearby, at our shop. We'll take you there—it's just a skip and hop." Fleng did a little jig, looking quite proud of his rhyme.

Katook said, "Of course I'd like to try your honey-dipped fruits, but only if you have enough."

"Enough?" said Plod with a laugh. "We have baskets overflowing with them."

"Just so. Let's go," the little anteater said impatiently.

"But wait," said Plod, "what about the grapes we came for?" He glanced at a beautiful bunch of purple grapes dangling from one of the rafters. "If we don't get them now, they'll go bad."

"But Plod, fat as you are, alas! You'll never get through that crowd without smooshing everyone you pass. And spiny as I am, oh dear! I'll never get through this crowd without pricking and poking everyone I near."

"If only we could fly over the crowd," mused Plod.

"I can do that," said Katook, wanting to help. "I can't exactly fly, but I can easily get those grapes without smooshing or poking anybody."

"I'll bet he could," Fleng said to Plod. "As easily as you or I dream we would."

"Of course I can!" said Katook, mesmerized by the grapes and eager to show off for his new friends. "But I don't have anything to give the merchant."

"Oh, don't worry about that. Here in Acco we pay later," Plod assured him.

Without another word, Katook jumped into the air. He grabbed on to an overhead beam and balanced a moment. "I'll be right back," he said, and began leaping from beam to beam.

Oh, how good this feels, thought Katook. *It's almost like being home again, leaping through the fig trees.*

Seconds later, Katook was perched above his prize. He smiled his thanks at the startled vendor then grabbed hold of the grapes and started back the way he'd come.

"Thief! Robber! Fruit absconder!" the merchant screamed.

Katook paused and looked back. The vendor was screaming at *him*!

"But—" Katook stammered. He never finished his explanation

because the merchant screamed, "I'll have your thieving paw!" and pulled out a long rusted sword from under his table. Waving the blade, the furious merchant ran after Katook.

"Hurry!" yelled Plod. "Toss the grapes!"

Fleng jumped up and down, waving his paws. "Our precious purple is near. Don't slow down because of fear!"

Confused, Katook swung faster and faster. He could hear the merchant yelling after him, and the sounds of the crowd below him. He felt a paw try to grab his leg. But Katook was quicker. He tossed the grapes to Fleng, then grabbed hold of Plod's long white tail as the gnu galloped away.

Plod kicked up his rear legs, knocking over a table and adding immeasurably to the market's chaos. Fleng had one fat little

paw curled around the grapes; with the other he held tight to Plod's mane. The cud-chewer galloped into the crowd, dragging Katook behind him.

Katook glanced over his shoulder. The merchant was chasing them, bouncing atop the back of an odd-looking rhinoceros, and threatening to use his blade on anyone who got in his way.

Plod ignored anything in his path. He trampled sacks of spices and sent a cloud of pepper in his wake, making both Katook and Fleng sneeze. He overturned a cart of eggs. Smashed a wagon of melons. Toppled a pyramid of perfectly balanced earthenware. And stomped on a large bladder filled with fish pudding that squirted right into the face of the angry merchant.

Fleng snickered as he looked back and saw the merchant slip and fall on the oily fish goo. Then, as Plod raced on in their mad escape, Fleng held up the grapes, as if taunting the little lemur. "Precious purple is here," Fleng crooned. "And soon you won't even be near."

"What do you mean?" Katook yelped, frightened and hanging on for dear life as Plod stampeded through a maze of twisted streets and alleys.

"You've been great fun, but our time together is done!" Fleng called.

Plod cut hard around a corner and through a narrow opening. Then he burst out of the town and onto a field of tall grass.

"Get off me!" snorted Plod.

"But—" started Katook, but that's all he managed to say, because Plod dipped his neck and furiously snapped his head back, sending Katook flying into the air . . .

Chapter Six
QUIGGA THE QUAGGA

Katook landed with a *thump* and an *ouch*, and the next thing he knew all was darkness. If it hadn't been for the hoof that woke him by not-too-gently nudging him in the head, he wondered how long he would have lain there. Or whether someone else would have found him—the angry merchant or someone even worse!

"Don't you have a better place to sleep?" a voice called down to him. "Look at you! What are you doing, lying in the middle of the grass like an unwashed pile of sleeping fur? Aren't you in the least concerned that you could trip some stunningly handsome quagga who's walking by, minding his own business?"

Katook rubbed his head and looked up and saw a four-legged animal staring haughtily down at him. The creature had a long face with large brown eyes and caramel stripes on a creamy hide that started at the tip of its nose and traveled past its dark mane before they disappeared halfway down its back. Katook thought it looked as if whoever started painting the stripes quit the job before finishing.

"Are you deaf as well as inconsiderate?" snorted the partly striped animal.

"I fell or, rather, I got thrown off—" Katook began.

"Well, which is it? Did you fall or get thrown? And if you were thrown, I'd like to know by whom, because I'd like to have a word with the fellow. It's disgraceful, tossing something living, or otherwise,

in the middle of a path for someone to trip over. What if I weren't as agile? I could have stepped on you and hurt myself."

"I'm sorry," said Katook, marveling at the strange way the creature talked to him.

"As you should be," the creature said as he made a wide, slow circle around Katook, limping slightly with each step.

"Your leg," Katook said, concerned. "Please tell me I didn't do that."

"Putting your head in my path certainly didn't help any. But no, I hurt myself stepping into a nasty little hole on a lovely, wide savannah that appeared absent of holes until I discovered perhaps the only one on the entire savannah."

"I'm sorry," said Katook, not knowing what else to say.

"Because of my strained foreleg, I've been temporarily detained from my herd who are, no doubt, days ahead of me. Leaving me to converse with the likes of you."

"If they're so far away, how will you find them?" asked Katook who, until recently, had never been away from his troop for even a day.

"I am a quagga," the creature answered grandly.

And though Katook knew that he'd be better off remaining silent rather than revealing his ignorance, he could no more hold a question in his mouth than expect the rain to fall upward.

"Why are you so sure you'll find your family?"

"Are you doubting me?" asked the quagga in a distinctly irritated tone.

"No, of course not," Katook answered quickly. "It's only that I'm far away from my home, and knowing how to find my kin seems like just the kind of trick I need to learn."

"It's a skill, not a trick. Clearly you've never met a quagga before."

"It's true, you're my first," Katook admitted.

"Well, if you had, you'd know that we are as a species known for our excellent sense of direction. Not only do we have a superior sense of knowing where we are and where we are going, but I, personally, am descended from a long line of quagga scouts. In fact, you are presently standing beneath the son of Quilla, son of Quiloz, son of Quiggoo from the Qualonia herd." Quigga whinnied to emphasize his point.

"Oh," said Katook, realizing he was supposed to be impressed. But the quagga names didn't mean anything to him. "You're very lucky to have an excellent sense of direction."

"And you evidently are not so lucky," said the quagga, tossing his mane again. "You're lost, aren't you?"

"Yes," confessed Katook. "But even if I knew my way home, I can't go back."

The quagga flared his nostrils and stared hard at Katook. "And why is that?" he asked. "What horrible thing did you do?"

Katook hesitated. He didn't want to tell the quagga about the curse of his blue eyes, so he merely said, "I saw what I shouldn't have seen."

"And what was that?" asked the quagga.

"I saw our priests eating the offering meant for another," Katook mumbled, unable to look the quagga in the eyes.

"Then the crime is theirs, not yours," the quagga proclaimed.

"But I went to the forbidden place," said Katook.

"You merely trespassed," said the quagga, sounding as if he were losing interest in Katook's story. "Is that it? Is that the extent of your crime?"

Katook was silent a moment, searching for words to describe how he felt when the Fossah loomed over him in the forest, and what he saw and the sensation he felt in the cave. But he couldn't find the words. It felt as though they were just out of his reach, like a name almost remembered.

"No, there's more," Katook said finally. "I can't say exactly what it was, but I suppose it was wrong to have seen it, or I'd still be with my family."

"If life were that simple." The quagga lowered his head and took a good, long look at Katook's face.

"What are you doing?" asked Katook nervously.

"What does it look like? I'm looking into your eyes."

Katook winced. "What do you see?"

"Beauty."

"In my eyes?" asked Katook, surprised.

"I know beauty," the quagga assured him. "She is a good friend of mine. That should be obvious in just looking at me. And as I look at your eyes…"

He's going to say I'm cursed, thought Katook.

"I suspect that you and beauty have more than a passing awareness of each other," the quagga went on. "Of course, you're clearly too ignorant to be aware of this."

But Katook was ashamed of his eyes and though he was thankful for the striped creature's almost kind words, he stared down at its hoofed feet.

"Don't look like that," ordered the quagga.

"Like what?" asked Katook, startled by his stern tone.

"Like you're ashamed of something. It's unbecoming and therefore I find it unenjoyable to behold."

Katook tried to look up into the quagga's proud, wide eyes, but found his gaze falling to his hoof. "Would you like me to wrap your leg?" asked Katook. "It will make it easier for you to walk. You might even be able to catch up to your herd."

"If you'd like." The quagga sounded as if he were the one doing Katook a favor. "But make it something attractive."

Katook gathered long flat pieces of grass, and with his nimble fingers and toes he braided them into a single band as long as his tail and as wide as his paw.

"My name is Katook." He knelt in front of the quagga. "What's yours?"

"I am Quigga. Son of—"

"Some very fine and beautiful creatures, I know," interrupted Katook. "Can I call you just Quigga?'

"Just Quigga? I suppose, if you must, but the truth is that I'm better known for speed, beauty and grace than for my ability to be just."

"I meant, may I only call you Quigga, instead of all the rest?"

"You may call me other things, too, as long as they are all complimentary."

Katook smiled and turned his attention to the bandage. Quigga's leg muscles twitched at Katook's slightest touch.

"Does it hurt?"

"Only when I walk."

"I'll be very gentle." But Quigga's leg muscled tightened even before Katook touched him. "No one has ever touched your leg before, have they?"

"Perhaps when I was a colt."

"Where I come from we touch each other all the time." Katook smiled to himself at the memory. "It's especially nice to be groomed by those who love you. High in a tree with the sun in your face and your eyes closed."

"Find me a nice warm pool of water and I'm capable of grooming myself, thank you very much."

Katook finished with the bandage. "There! See how that feels."

Quigga took a step, lifting his leg high and then setting it down carefully. "How does it look?"

"It's not too tight?"

"It doesn't clash with my stripes, does it?"

Katook had no idea what Quigga meant, but he sensed that he knew the right answer. "It looks perfect."

Quigga reared up on his back legs and kicked his forelegs out in front of him to get a better look at Katook's handiwork.

"So, then, I'm off. To dilly is to delay rejoining my herd."

"It's dally, I think," replied Katook.

"Dilly, dally, call it what you will, but I must go. Thank you for my anklet."

"You're welcome," Katook said, but in his heart he wished that Quigga wouldn't leave him there all alone.

Silently he watched Quigga walk away. *What will become of me now?* he wondered. *I can't go back to Acco, at least not without getting blamed for stealing what I didn't mean to steal. And I can't stay here just waiting for someone else to come along and kick me in the head.*

"Can I come with you?" Katook called out.

Quigga turned. "With me?"

"Travel with you. Just until you rejoin your herd. Maybe on the way I'll find others like myself. But until then we'll have each other."

Quigga slowly walked back to Katook and silently circled him—twice. "Before I consider your request any further, I want to make something very clear."

"Of course."

"*With me* does not mean *on me,*" the Quagga said.

"I can walk on my own," Katook assured him.

"Stumble, hop, skip, do whatever you like, but don't count on ever gracing my majestic back with your furry bottom. Is this very clear?"

"Yes," said Katook, who was beginning to wonder what kind of traveling companion Quigga would turn out to be. "I promise I won't ride you."

The quagga gave a heavy sigh. "I suppose there are worse things than being seen with a fat-fingered furry-handed runt like you. Besides, when my bandage needs attending you might come in handy, if you'll excuse the pun."

"Wonderful," said Katook, relieved. "Let's go."

Quigga pointed his nose toward the sun. He closed his eyes and inhaled deeply. He circled twice in place, then stopped, opened his eyes and stared across a wide grassy field. Without bothering to glance at Katook, he proclaimed with absolute certainty, "This way."

And so off they went, their backs to Acco, Katook walking in the shade of his new companion.

The sun was warm on their backs as they crossed the dry yellow flatlands that surrounded Acco and began a long, gradual ascent toward what Quigga described as "the right way." As they continued up the gentle slope, the grasses turned from pale green to a rich, deep emerald that reminded Katook of home.

"I've never been anywhere before," Katook told Quigga, who walked beside him.

Quigga was silent. He walked with his head high, his eyes staring straight ahead. Katook noticed how Quigga's nostrils flared from time to time. He imagined that he was inhaling familiar aromas from far away—smells leading them in the right direction.

"I mean, I've been places," continued Katook. "I've just never been anyplace outside of Kattakuk. That's the name of the place where I'm from."

"Never heard of it," replied Quigga. "And I've seen a great deal of the world, believe me."

"I think you'd like it. Not now, I mean, because it's very cold and everyone's hungry. But someday, when the sun returns, oh, you should see it—the way the light shines through the fig leaves and makes everything a beautiful golden-green."

"I hate trees," said Quigga. "But the light does sound flattering."

"You would look very handsome in that light," Katook assured him.

Quigga glanced down at Katook, and as Katook looked up into the quagga's eyes he thought he saw kindness in them. For a moment he didn't feel so alone. "Will you be my friend?" Katook asked.

"Your friend?" repeated Quigga.

"Will you be the one I can talk to when I feel like I have to talk to someone?" explained Katook. "Of course, being your friend doesn't mean I can climb on your back. But it would be nice to feel like I could even though I never will."

They walked in silence a moment or two, and then Quigga said quietly, "I will be your friend."

And that was all that needed to be said for a great while.

Late that afternoon they stopped at a small pond. Katook sat on a rock and watched fat white clouds skim across the water's surface and then suddenly ripple apart as Quigga dipped his muzzle into the pond. Katook knelt beside his new friend, and together they drank the sweet springwater. When Katook had quenched his thirst, he wiped his face with his paws.

Clean and refreshed, he turned to ask Quigga how

much farther they had to go, but Quigga was already walking away.

Katook hurried to catch up. He was almost beside him when he heard the dry sound of feathers slicing through the air. Looking up, he saw a hawk diving straight at him, its talons flared wide open.

Katook tumbled in the soft grass. The hawk struck the ground directly behind him, let out an angry, frustrated *squawk*, then soared into the sky for another attack. Katook ran toward Quigga and, just as the hawk arced for another strike, Katook dived under the quagga's haunches and hid there, his heart thumping madly in his chest.

"What are you doing?" demanded Quigga, his neck craned under him as he looked at Katook huddled beneath his belly. "It's just a bird."

Katook sheepishly peered past Quigga's spindly legs. Now the hawk was circling lazily in the blue sky.

"But . . . ," started Katook, then suddenly grew silent at the sight of a large brilliantly colored diamond of light dancing across the meadow and stopping a short distance away. The diamond of light was violet, then turned molten orange, then fiery red, and finally a soft honeysuckle yellow as it settled lightly on Quigga's hoof. It flickered there, slowly turning colors.

"Don't move," whispered Katook, mesmerized by the jewel of light.

"Why," Quigga demanded, alarmed. "What's wrong now?"

"Just don't move," urged Katook as he slowly reached out to catch the light in his paws. But the moment he was about to touch it, the diamond slid off Quigga's hoof and skimmed across the meadow. Katook followed it with his eyes as it raced across the thick, green grass without leaving a trace, then started climbing a small rise. That's when Katook heard the laughter.

57

He looked up and saw the hawking party—three robed colobus monkeys, one riding on a giant sable and two on bluebok antelopes. A hawk swooped down and settled on the leather-wrapped forearm of one of the monkeys. Then Katook noticed the fist-sized crystal clutched in the paw of one of the other nobles. By turning the crystal just so, the monkey moved the colorful shapes that poured out of the clear stone—sending them back across the grass and onto Katook's chest.

Katook grabbed for the purple diamond that was sliding along his stomach.

"You cannot grasp a slice of light, silly creature," said the monkey. She tucked her crystal into a pocket hidden in the thick folds of her robe, and the purple diamond disappeared.

"I was just playing with it," said Katook, a little defensively.

"Of course you were," replied the monkey. "Please, allow us to introduce ourselves. We are of the Kolloboo. My name is Alliptas; this is Furoz." She pointed to the one who rode beside her. He was staring at his own crystal, lost in thought.

"And I am Balway," said the third, who held the hawk.

58

"We can break apart the sunlight," said Furoz
distractedly. "But we can't seem to put it back together again."

"Why break it in the first place?" asked Katook.

The Kolloboo all looked at each other, perplexed by the question.

"Because we can," answered Balway.

"Because we must," answered Furoz.

"If we didn't, how would we understand how it works?" asked Alliptas.

"But do you have to break something to know how it works?"
asked Katook.

"If you don't break it, you at least have to take it apart," began
Balway. "If not, how else can you measure it? Know its purpose?
Its direction? Its very reason for being?"

"I can't speak for the other things," Quigga said, "but as for direction,
I don't need to break anything to know which way is which, and which
way isn't. I simply close my eyes and smell the air."

"Of course you do," said Balway skeptically.

"But you could just as easily use one of these," said Furoz as
he pulled a small, round wooden box from under his cloak.

"What is it?" asked Katook.

"Come here and I'll show you," answered the monkey.

Quigga hung back but Katook rushed over to look at the mysterious little box. It was lined with mother-of-pearl. In the very center of the box a single, jet-black, needle-sized bar was suspended on a pin. Furoz turned the box, but no matter which way he turned it, the bar remained pointing in the same direction.

"What is it?" asked Katook.

"We call it a needle-guide," answered Alliptas. "We use it to find our way," she explained.

"How does it work?" asked Katook. "And why does it always point the same way?"

"We don't know that yet, but in time we will," Furoz answered.

"Can you show me how to use it?" asked Katook as he held the box very carefully in his paws.

"Why waste your time?" said Quigga haughtily. "You have no need for silly little boxes to find your way. You have me."

"Of course I have you. It's just that—"

"Put it on the ground," interrupted Quigga.

Katook did as he was asked. He carefully set the needle-guide in front of Quigga then asked, "Is that all right?"

"Perfect," replied Quigga. He stared at it a moment, then suddenly lifted his hoof and stepped squarely down on top of the box, shattering it.

"Quigga!" yelled Katook, horrified. "Look what you've done!"

"Oops," said Quigga innocently. He turned to the monkeys. "But then I suppose you should thank me. Now that it's broken, perhaps you'll be able to understand it better. As for finding one's direction," he added with a flip of his mane, "I'm quite content with my nose."

Horribly embarrassed by his friend's behavior, Katook turned to the Kolloboo and said, "Please forgive him. He's very proud, and well—"

"Do not worry," interrupted Alliptas. "We have many more needle-guides at the castle. And your friend is absolutely correct when he says that someday we will understand how it works. Someday we will know how everything works."

What a strange thing to say, thought Katook. Then, for a reason beyond reason, Katook remembered the Fossah. He recalled the feelings of wonder and mystery he had felt in his presence. *Not everything can be understood,* he thought.

"Don't you think some mysteries are better left that way?" Katook wondered aloud.

The Kolloboo looked at each other then broke out in laughter.

"You are a wonderful little creature with a marvelous sense of humor!" said Furoz, giving Katook a playful slap on his back.

"Come, join us," said Balway. "We're on our way to Hatipha Hold now."

"Hatipha Hold?"

"The castle," Alliptas explained, "and the center for all our studies."

From a distance the castle seemed to be made of a hundred spires of roughly poured mud. The slender earth-colored spikes pierced the blue sky.

"Oh, my," Katook said in awe.

"Yes," answered Alliptas, who looked as if she enjoyed the wonder in Katook's eyes.

"It is so beautiful," Katook said. "Quigga, have you ever seen anything so amazing?"

But Quigga remained stubbornly silent.

If the sight of those unearthly spires didn't impress Quigga, Katook knew that the first comment he heard upon entering the castle surely did.

"What stunning lines on that horselike creature!" They all turned to see a Kolloboo whose eyes were locked on Quigga's front legs. "Exquisite!" the Kolloboo continued. "Alliptas, where did you find such an amazing animal? And will you please hurry and introduce me to it!"

"This is Fansera," Alliptas explained to Katook and Quigga. "Fansera is our most celebrated artist."

"Pah!" exclaimed the artist. "I merely paint what I see. But what I see in this stunning beast inspires me. And I'm sure it will inspire my students, as well. May I detain you?" he implored the quagga.

Katook looked to Quigga, who seemed to be doing his best to appear disinterested. It was clear to Katook, though, that his friend was flattered by the artist's praise and would like nothing better than to pose for him and his students.

"Quigga," began Katook, "it's fine with me, if you wouldn't mind."

"Well, I suppose," said Quigga. Then he turned to face Fansera. "Lead the way."

Katook smiled to himself at just how easily the quagga's moods swayed.

A short time later, in a room filled with tall, bright windows, eight Kolloboo stood behind eight large easels. Each of them was staring at Quigga, who posed for them. He had gold ribbons woven into his mane and silver ribbons braided through his tail. Katook could tell by the way Quigga kept blinking his long eyelashes that he was very pleased with himself and the way he looked.

Alliptas came up beside Katook. "Would you like to see the map room?"

Katook turned to Quigga. "I won't be long."

"There is a lot of beauty for these fine artists to capture," said Quigga. "Take your time. I feel confident they will need it."

What happens when one sees something so far beyond one's understanding that there are no words for it? Like a baby lemur's first taste of a fresh fig after a diet of only its mother's milk. Is the kit shocked by that first sweet taste of fig? No, the first taste is simply "other." In fact, that first taste is so "other" that it leaves the kit breathless. This is what Katook felt as he entered the map room and gazed up at a map as tall as a tree and as wide as a banyan grove.

The wall was covered with shapes and colors and names, nut-brown mountain ranges, blue seas, green plains, and umber deserts.

"These are places?" he asked quietly.

"Drawings of places," answered Alliptas. "This is Katurrah, the world as we know it."

"Can I see my home?" Katook asked.

"Of course," said Alliptas. "What is the name of this place?"

"It's called Bo-hibba," answered Katook.

"Did you hear him?" Alliptas called up to the Keeper of the Map, who stood on a tall ladder, a paintbrush in his paw as he worked on a serpent of some kind.

"It doesn't exist," the Keeper of the Map called down to them.

"But it's my home," insisted Katook.

"Perhaps," replied the Keeper of the Map. "But we do not have it yet. Perhaps it is to the far south, but more likely the far north."

"What is the north?" asked Katook, concerned.

"It is where the map vanishes and exploration begins," answered Alliptas.

"Do you suppose there are others like me in this north?" asked Katook.

"It's possible."

"Well, then do you know how to find this north? Because there is nothing I want more than to find others like me," said Katook.

"I see," Alliptas replied thoughtfully. "There are three things that will help you. First, take this." She handed Katook a needle-guide she pulled from her cloak. "It insists upon always pointing to the north. Second, we will get you a map from the library. And third, you must find Nadab."

"Nadab?" repeated Katook.

"Nadab is our finest explorer. She has traveled from one end of Katurrah to the other. Much of what you see on this map is the result of her explorations. If there is anyone who can help you find those like yourself, it is Nadab."

"Can I talk to her?" Katook asked eagerly.

"Once you find her," Alliptas replied. "Nadab is not among the Kolloboo. She is in Og Ashad, the city of the Golden Monkeys." Alliptas pointed to a drawing of a city near the very top of the great map. "Now come with me."

Alliptas led Katook to an enormous room she called the library. It was filled with objects called "books," which stood on shelves as high as Katook could see. Katook noticed how each book seemed to have its own special place, as tens of Kolloboo attended the books, placing them carefully on the shelves. Overseeing this activity was the Master of Records, an elderly monkey who sat cross-legged on a high stool, his watery eyes lost in a large bound volume.

"Are the books hollow inside, like boxes?" Katook wondered aloud.

Alliptas smiled, "They're like boxes in that they hold things inside them. But they hold stories and memories, not objects. Each book is like a silent storyteller just waiting to be prompted to tell its tale."

Alliptas took down a book and opened it. She ran her thumb across the pages, and Katook marveled how they fanned, like delicate leaves.

"Here, look at this page," said Alliptas as she paused over a single leaf.

Katook could see tiny marks all over it but could hear no story.

"Those are words," explained Alliptas. "And we are on our way to put some of those words on a special object you can take with you, so that when you meet Nadab the words will tell her who you are and what you're looking for."

"I could tell her myself," said Katook, confused.

"Yes, but this way she'll know you came from us. And she will know you better because of it."

Katook didn't understand what Alliptas meant by this but remained silent.

"But first let's see if we can find a sketch of one of your kind in the journals Nadab sent us from the land of the Golden Monkeys."

Alliptas called up to the head librarian with a formal bow. "Master, do you know if Nadab has found an animal such as this one standing beside me?"

The Master of the Records turned his slow, liquid gaze on Katook, then called out to one of his underlings, "Bring me spring, five cycles ago."

Almost as soon as the last word escaped his mouth, one of the librarians-in-training pulled a heavy, weather-worn journal from a shelf and hurried it over to the Master of Records. Katook watched as the elder expertly slid one finger into the large book and opened it exactly to the page he was looking for. "Yes," the librarian murmured to himself. Then he crooked a finger at Katook, who quickly scampered up the stool and peered over his shoulder.

Katook stared with amazement, because magically scratched across the page, in vivid black and white, was the image of an animal who indeed looked so much like Katook that his heart beat faster. "Are you sure that it was Nadab herself who captured the image of this animal?"

"None other," replied the Master of Records. Then he slammed the journal shut in an explosion of golden dust and turned back to his book.

"Come," said Alliptas. "Let us prepare you for Nadab."

Katook followed her out of the library. They walked down a long hallway toward the Master Scribe, a very slender Kolloboo who was hunched over a wide workbench, carefully arranging an assortment of tools that were spread out before him.

Behold a sketch of an inhabitant of Lothal heretofore unknown to us. A more complete description of this race shall be sent in my next epistle.

Ego, Naturabimus, meet with the under-chatel on the more their tailes re Ringed with darker Bandes

Katook watched Alliptas bow to the Master Scribe then enter
a small room where a block of moist red clay sat on a pedestal.

"Neat, neat, neat," the Master Scribe called after them.
"Keep it clean, keep it orderly, make it legible!"

"Yes, Master," Alliptas answered through the open doorway.
She tore a small chunk of clay from the block and rolled it until it was
very flat and about the size of Katook's nose. Then she used a pointed
stick to make tiny marks in the soft clay—marks that looked like
the ones Katook had just seen in the books. Finally, she rolled the flat
piece of clay around the stick and left it to dry in a bar of sunlight
on a windowsill.

They stayed in that small, quiet room and talked awhile, each of
them sitting in a simple chair around an old wooden table. Alliptas
was a great listener and very curious about Katook's travels. By the
time Katook told her all he had seen, the clay seal had hardened
and dried. Alliptas removed the stick from the center of the seal.
Then she found a cord in her robes and looped it through the seal,
as if it were a large bead.

"Here," said Alliptas, handing it to Katook. "You must give this
to Nadab when you find her. Now put it on."

Katook slipped the cord over his neck and felt the small cylinder
rest against his heart. "Where is this place?" he asked. "This land of the
Golden Monkeys."

Alliptas slid a map across the table and smoothed it open with
her paws. "It is here," she said, pointing to a tiny castle on the map.
"You will know the monkeys by the rich, golden luster of their fur."

Katook neatly folded the map and tucked it away. "Do you really
think I will find this Nadab?" he asked uncertainly and a bit afraid
of the answer she might give him.

"I believe anything is possible," replied Alliptas.

When Katook returned to the art studio, the sun had dropped
below the large windows, flooding the room in a burnt-orange light.
Quigga remained as statuesque and content as when Katook had left
him hours before. His golden-laced tail still jutted importantly straight
out behind him, and his head hadn't dipped in the least.

"Katook," Quigga called to him. "Take a peek for me, won't you?
See how well they've captured the beauty that is me."

Katook walked behind the semicircle of easels and peered over
the painters' shoulders as they worked. He started at one end and
worked his way down the line. What he saw made him smile.
Not because the artists had painted Quigga in a funny manner. Quite
the opposite; the paintings were very serious. One artist was painting
a detail of Quigga's neck, another was painting a study of Quigga's
right thigh, while a third was working on a close-up of the little fuzzy
stubble that sprouted just below Quigga's mouth.

"Well?" Quigga said impatiently. "Do their paintings portray my true beauty?"

Katook squinted at the canvases, trying to think of the right thing to say.

"Poetry, my thick-thumbed friends," continued Quigga. "I am prepared for visual poetry. I am looking forward to dropping to my knees in sheer delight."

"Oh, you'll drop to your knees, Quigga," said Katook. "I'm pretty sure of that."

Quigga abandoned his pose and strutted around to join Katook. But the instant he saw the first painting—a detail of the fuzzy hairs under his chin—he reared up and let out a shrieking whinny. He galloped down the line, his eyes bulging in horror as he stared at one painting after the next.

"What is this ugliness?" he screamed. "You've torn me apart!"

"We call it science," one of the painters responded calmly.

"You've destroyed beauty and replaced it with meaningless scraps of nothingness," Quigga ranted. "This isn't art. This is . . . it's—"

"Science," explained another painter.

"Science being the stronger hand of art," continued the first.

"This is how we understand things. We call it the pursuit of knowledge."

"Knowledge?" Quigga shrieked, his voice echoing in the cavernous hall. "Science! You can't 'know' something better by destroying it!"

Quigga turned his back on the paintings and suddenly bucked his rear legs, sending a sharp hoof through a portrait of his ear. He continued down the line of easels, expertly punching a hole in each of the canvases.

Quigga stopped for a moment, a look of satisfaction on his face. Then he galloped from the studio, yelling over his shoulder, "Away! I refuse to spend another moment with these—these artistic butchers!"

Katook turned to the artists. "I'm so sorry—"

Alliptas calmly interrupted him. "It is not your fault."

"But look what he's done!" said Katook. He didn't know what to do. He was afraid that if he didn't leave at once, Quigga would run so fast and so far that he might never find him again. And he was afraid that if he did leave now, the Kolloboo, who had been so kind, would think him ungrateful.

"It is to be understood," Alliptas told him. "Some are meant to know, others are simply meant to be. Your friend is like that. He doesn't care to understand things, only to live."

"What about me? Which am I?" asked Katook, curious once more.

"You treasure both," Alliptas answered simply. And the artists bobbed their heads in agreement. "Go, now. Hurry after your friend."

"Thank you for my gifts," Katook said.

"They are merely tools," responded Alliptas. "Let us hope that Nadab can deliver you to your true gift—"

"Others like me," said Katook, finishing Alliptas's thought.

"Knowledge," Alliptas corrected him. "And, yes, others like you, too," she added with a smile.

With the map and the needle-guide in a pouch slung over his shoulder, and the clay seal thumping against his heart as he ran, Katook hurried after Quigga.

67

Chapter Eight
CITY OF THE DEAD

The sun burned Katook's eyes. His mouth was dry, his lips caked with dust. He trudged onward. The scorching heat spread out across the desert like a molten pool of sand that turned even the blue on the horizon into waves of rolling vapor.

The little lemur squinted up at the sky and silently pleaded with the merciless sun to pull away, to cool, to turn dark, to do anything but continue scorching him with its heat. He had never felt so hopeless.

Does the Fossah watch over these barren lands, too? Katook wondered. *And if he does, is this part of my punishment for seeing what I should never have seen?*

"This is where I'll die," he muttered to himself.

"Not another word," ordered Quigga, who was walking three lengths ahead.

"It's true."

"It's *not* my truth, so keep it to yourself."

They crossed the desert for three days, but for Katook they melted together into one burning, endless day. He tried to ignore his thirst and the blisters on the pads of his paws.

Still, there was no help for it, he told himself. He had to keep going. To somehow lift one burning paw off the scorching sand, shuffle it forward, then continue with the next. Over and over again. He thought: *Keep going. Don't stop. Lift. Step.*

After the first day, Katook and Quigga hardly spoke to each other. What's there to say? Katook thought. *We're both miserable. I have to trust that Quigga knows where he's going. Besides, there's no turning back, and one direction seems as good, or as terrible, as the next.*

The heat became unbearable. It hurt even to breathe. Katook tried desperately to think of other things. Cool things. Shade. Icy stones. Even the chill of water. But no matter how hard he tried, the heat found its way into his thoughts, which seemed to blur and lose shape as soon as they were formed.

Katook saw a line of giraffes, taller than the tallest trees, marching alongside him. Tens of the long-necked creatures moving soundlessly across the desert.

He started to call out to Quigga, to tell him about the giraffes, but Quigga was many lengths ahead and Katook's mouth was too dry to yell.

That's when Katook realized the giraffes weren't marching. In fact, they weren't even moving. They were carved into a great wall of stone, monumental in scale.

70

A parade of animals as lifeless as I will soon be, he thought.

Late in the afternoon on the third day, with Quigga walking beside him, Katook heard a voice. "They look thirsty."

Katook and Quigga stopped and looked around, but there was no one there.

"How 'bout we show 'em where the water lives," continued the voice.

"Quigga?" Kataook managed to say.

"Yes, I hear it, too."

Two black crows landed directly in front of them. The birds cocked their heads and looked at each other. The larger of the two hopped forward, aimed his sulfur-yellow eyes up at Katook, and said, "You and your friend look very thirsty."

"We are," whispered Katook through parched lips.

"Would you like to drink?" the crow asked pleasantly.

"Oh, yes, please," Katook almost begged.

"Then why don't you?" said the crow, and he and his partner broke out in cackling laughter and flew away.

Katook started frantically digging in the sand. "Is it here? Is this where the water lives?" he called after the crows.

"There's no water," said Quigga. "They were being cruel. It's what crows do."

But Katook was mad from the heat and kept digging, burning his fingers and muttering, "The water lives here. I just need to find it. Maybe if I just dig deeper—"

"Get up, Katook," Quigga said.

"But the water—"

"There is no water."

"But—"

"Stand up and climb on my back. I'll carry you," Quigga said gently.

Katook stopped digging. He stared up at his friend and shook his head, because he knew that this was not done. Quigga had made that clear. Besides, he had promised.

"Don't make me say it twice." Quigga knelt in the sand so that Katook could climb onto his back.

Katook paused, not quite believing what he was seeing, then slowly he pulled himself onto Quigga's shoulders and settled on his striped back.

"Thank you," he said into his friend's ear. "Thank you," he repeated even more softly.

They traveled like that all day and all night. Katook fell asleep, his face buried in Quigga's soft mane. He woke to the soft yellow-gray of early morning. A light breeze carried the faint fragrance of flowers. Katook rubbed his paws across his dry, crusty eyes, stunned to see that Quigga was carrying him toward a spring that was crowded with birds—crows, rooks, ravens, and magpies—all of them greedily drinking from a pool of pale blue water.

"Drink what you may, you will die anyway," raged a rook.

"Get away!" cawed a crow.

"The desert is vast, we'll have your carcasses at last!" railed a raven.

Quigga ignored their taunts and shoved his way through their beating wings. He made his way to the base of the spring, then bent over the clear water and drank his fill.

Katook hopped down and knelt beside his friend and drank and drank until he could drink no more. He was just about to wash the dust from his face when the birds suddenly lifted off, and he caught the pungent odor of Quigga's fear.

"Quigga . . . ?"

"It's coming," said Quigga, his voice choked with fright. "Quickly, get back on!"

"What are you talking about?" asked Katook.

"That . . . ," Quigga said, jutting his nose to the north.

Katook sat up tall on Quigga's shoulders and looked toward where he was pointing. It looked like a distant curtain of shade that seemed to be racing from the northern horizon straight at them. In seconds it had blocked the sun and turned the sky a dirty brown.

"What is it?" he asked.

"Pain" was all Quigga said, then he spun his body around in place, his eyes searching madly for shelter. "All we can do is hope I can outrun it."

"Outrun *what* to *where*?"

The light breeze suddenly turned into a fierce wind that grew steadily stronger as the dark curtain advanced.

72

because the hissing sand obscured its shape, making it look faint and ghostlike.

Quigga turned and raced toward the city. And the full raging power of the sandstorm came down on them. The dirty sky turned even darker. The sound of the wind grew shrill. The violent whistling hurt inside Katook's head. His ears were flattened against his head, his eyes squeezed shut. He hunched over, his belly tight against Quigga's back. Then he screamed.

Quigga blindly galloped through an arched, gateless entry and into a huge empty courtyard. The sandstorm chased after them. Sand tore into their skin.

"We've got to get out of the open!" Quigga screamed over the wind.

They raced toward an alley that broke from the courtyard and disappeared into darkness. Quigga hated entering the dark, cramped place, but they had no choice.

Moments later Katook felt Quigga's muscles relax just a bit as the dark, narrow alley opened onto a wide plaza. Katook blinked at the strange sight before them. The plaza was filled with massive statues, toppled and ruined by the wind. Quigga galloped toward the nearest one, and they found shelter in a niche beneath the belly of the great stone beast.

Gasping, Quigga stood, legs trembling, rump braced against the stone behind him. Katook slipped off Quigga's back and huddled between his forelegs.

"What a strange place this is," whispered Quigga, slowly closing his eyes. "I don't think anyone's lived here for a long time."

Katook squinted through the windblown sand. He gazed up at black and empty windows. He stared down the plaza as far as he could but saw only darkness.

"Someone lives here," Katook said ominously.

Quigga's eyes parted. He looked at Katook. "Why do you say that? There's not a light in a window, not a snake of smoke from a chimney. This place has been deserted for years. It's . . . dead."

"Don't you smell it?" asked Katook.

"No, my nostrils are clogged with sand." Quigga sneezed violently.

Katook was hesitant. He didn't want to make Quigga any more frightened than he already was.

"Hang on!" yelled Quigga over the howling wind. He started galloping, his back to the onrushing wall of darkness.

"Where are we going?" Katook called out.

"Anywhere but here."

That's when the first wave of the sandstorm hit them. It was like a swarm of insects stinging all at once. The sand burned their eyes and blasted their skin in a wash of pain.

Katook clung tightly to Quigga's neck as the quagga ran into the stinging furnace of wind and sand. The sound was deafening, the bite of the sand worse than fire. Katook could feel Quigga's hooves pounding the desert, but he couldn't hear a thing over the screaming wind.

"Quigga, over there!" yelled Katook. "I think I see a city!"

"You're imagining things," gasped Quigga.

"But it is. I'm sure of it. To your right! Run to your right!"

The city was almost impossible to see. Not only because it was made of dun-colored sandstone that blended into the desert, but also

Quigga's velvety nose wrinkled. He sneezed again, and then his eyes widened. "It's—"

"Blood" was all Katook said.

The sandstorm raged all through the night. Quigga somehow managed to drift off to sleep, but Katook lay there in the dark listening to the hissing of the wind. Suddenly he heard another sound: a faint, guttural growling.

Katook shivered. With the wind still blowing dark plumes of sand, he couldn't be sure the shadowy shapes he saw in the distance were real. Then he heard the growling again, sounding closer this time. Whatever they were, Katook sensed they were moving through the abandoned streets, drawn from their lairs by the scent of his fear.

"Quigga, wake up," whispered Katook, his voice quivering.

"What is it?"

"Shhh." He put a paw on Quigga's smooth flank. "Don't move."

Quigga's ears pricked. He clearly heard them coming, too. His large, dark eyes became wide with fear, and his jaw trembled ever so slightly.

At the edge of the plaza Katook caught a fleeting glimpse of something moving. It slunk low to the ground, gliding back and forth like a dark cloud, coming closer. Then, through the darkness and the shifting sand, he saw another. And another.

"Bone-crushers," Quigga whispered, his body trembling.

"Many," Katook whispered, watching the giant wolflike creatures.

Katook felt Quigga try to back against the wall for safety, but his flanks were already pressed to the stone. There was nowhere to go.

75

Suddenly a masked face pushed through the windblown sands, a gleaming sword held high.

"Get up!" ordered a muffled voice.

"W-who are you?" asked Katook, wondering which was worse: the bone-crushers or the stranger with the sword.

"No time for that. Get up!"

Katook felt his body shaking with fear and regret. It was all his fault. None of this would be happening—the sandstorm, the bone-crushers, this stranger with the sword—if it wasn't for the curse of his blue eyes. He knew what he had to do.

"Please, take me," said Katook, trying to sound brave. "But leave my friend alone. He hasn't done anything wrong. It's me you want."

At that instant one of the bone-crushers leapt. Katook saw its gaping mouth, its jagged teeth, and its flared, outstretched claws. Katook screamed as Quigga reared up, his forelegs flailing. But it was the stranger's sword hurtling through the air that met the creature. His blade sliced into the bone-crusher's neck. The beast fell, its already dead eyes staring straight at Katook as if to say: *You were mine.*

"Get on your feet," the stranger commanded. "We don't have much time."

Quigga nodded to Katook, and the little lemur scrambled up onto his back. With their masked rescuer brandishing his sword to stave off the bone-crushers, they followed him out beyond the city walls.

"Who are you?" Katook yelled over the wind as eight more dark, hulking shapes emerged from the darkness. All of them were hooded, swathed in robes, and riding large desert antelopes. One of them handed the reins of an antelope to Katook and Quigga's rescuer, who mounted it and rode off, the others trailing him.

Katook and Quigga fell in behind the cloaked figures, following the antelopes away from the dead city and back into the storm.

Despite the wind, the antelopes set a swift pace. Katook felt his fear growing stronger. Who were these strangers and where were they taking them? He desperately wished that someone would at least slow down and talk to them, but the forbidding strangers rode harder, the antelopes crossing the desert in great, graceful strides.

At last the antelopes slowed their pace and Quigga drew even with the lead rider.

Katook spoke up, his heart pounding. "Excuse me, sir."

The stranger cocked his head. But he didn't respond.

Katook swallowed and tried again. "How did you know, sir, where we were?" Katook's fur stood on end as the rider continued to regard him. Then a paw reached out to unwind a bit of cloak, and the white-muzzled face of a red-furred monkey appeared. "My name is Hasara. We are the Patah. Not a grain of sand can shift in our desert, nor a creature walk among us without our knowing."

"Pretty sure of himself, isn't he," whispered Quigga to Katook.

"And there's not a sound that can be made that we won't hear," said Hasara with an edge in his voice that silenced any further mutterings.

As quickly as the storm had arrived, it departed. The wind vanished. The night sky was clear and pierced with stars. It seemed to Katook that Hasara looked at them not with wonder, but with a kind of purpose, as if they somehow spoke to him.

"Sir . . . please . . . what do you see?" asked Katook, his fear warring with curiosity.

"My place under the heavens. And with that I find my direction."

"Direction?" This interested Katook, who had been feeling rather lost ever since the sandstorm. "The Kolloboo gave me a needle-guide," he explained to Hasara, "but Quigga leads our way."

"I'm not only talking about which way to travel," said Hasara. "Direction is both inside and outside of us."

"But how can you know where you're going if you stare at the stars, and not at the ground in front of you?" asked Katook.

Hasara pointed a finger at the stars. "Do you see that sapphire-blue star sitting in that small ruby cluster? And do you see the line formed by those very bright stars over there?"

"I think so," Katook said uncertainly.

"They're our guides," said Hasara. "Here in the desert, the land shifts with the winds but the stars remain constant. If we depended on the ground in front of us, as you suggest, we'd be as lost as you are."

Katook had never thought about the night sky this way. Back home, the trees showed him the way, but here, he realized, there weren't any trees.

"The stars are everything," Hasara continued as if he heard Katook's thoughts.

"Will you teach me?" Katook asked.

"There's no need for this nonsense," interjected Quigga. "You're with me." Quigga flipped back his mane and gazed coolly at Hasara. "Though it may be difficult for you stargazers to understand, I can find my way with my eyes closed."

Hasara looked at Quigga a moment, then turned, called something to the other riders in a language Katook didn't understand, and continued riding.

They crossed the desert mostly in silence, but from time to time they'd stop and Hasara would teach Katook how to read the stars. He showed him how to see the pelican carrying the elephant in the stars, and the lion, and the rabbit with the eel tail. But whenever they stopped, Quigga would walk away from them and fix his gaze on the horizon, wearing an expression of supreme disinterest.

After they had gone some distance, they cleared a small rise. Katook looked down and saw a firelit encampment. It seemed to be made of a circle of huge boulders covered by one vast golden canopy. The canopy looked like a softly lit cloud that had settled onto the desert.

"Is that your home?" Katook asked.

"No." Hasara waved his arm across the black expanse around them.

"This is my home. My home is where I sleep, and where I sleep is where I set my tent."

"But where do you set your tent?" asked Katook, confused.

"I set it where I sleep," said Hasara with the first hint of a smile.

"But you must have some idea of where you are going," said Quigga impatiently.

"Why should I? If there's water and food and the embrace of my kin, is one place better than the next?"

"Then why move at all? Why not just keep your tents where they are?" asked Katook.

"What?" said Hasara. "And consider myself wiser than the stars that cross the sky? No. We Patah move with from place to place because we follow the stars. That is our nature." Here Hasara turned his attention toward Quigga. "Only fools believe themselves more important than their nature. Wouldn't you agree, wind-drinker?"

Quigga gazed off toward the camp, as if he had far better things to do than reply to Hasara. But Katook kept his gaze on the stars and wondered if it was his nature to wander like the Patah, or whether he was meant for another life—a life that suited his own nature, whatever that might be.

Chapter Nine
THE PATAH

Quigga, with Katook still on his back, followed the riders toward the low ridge of boulders that surrounded the Patah camp. Abruptly, Hasara stopped and held up a paw. Katook and Quigga exchanged a confused glance. Hasara made a strange guttural clicking sound with his tongue. Suddenly, inexplicably, the ridge moved!

Katook pulled Quigga back in fright as they watched the berm slowly part. Where seconds before a wall of great rocks had stood, there was now an opening wide enough for the riders to pass through.

"Come," said Hasara as the antelope he rode started through the gap.

"Did you see that?" Katook murmured to Quigga. "I mean, did you see that?"

"Shhh!" ordered Hasara.

Cautiously, Quigga stepped onto the newly formed path. But a few steps later he froze in terror. The ridge surrounding the camp was alive! It was actually a circle of giant, sleeping, armored beasts, each one resting its armored head on the macelike tail of the one in front of it in one long continuous circle. The opening had been made when one of these enormous creatures moved forward slightly.

"Quietly now," Hasara said softly. "They've worked hard today. Let them sleep."

Katook gave Quigga's neck an encouraging pat, and Quigga hurried through the narrow gap and into the encampment. The instant he made it through, the mountainous creature groggily moved back into place, let out a loud, foul-smelling fart, and promptly fell fast asleep.

"What was that?" Katook whispered to Quigga, holding his nose from the stench.

"A glyptodont," answered Hasara. "We care for them, and they protect us."

"From the bone-crushers?" asked Katook.

"Yes, them and, well . . . others," he responded mysteriously.

Katook and Quigga now found themselves beneath the golden canopy, inside what felt like a very large tent. A faint smell of spices hung in the air. Candles and oil lamps flickered against walls of saffron, burgundy, and azure fabric. The tent was filled to bursting with Patah and antelope-folk, all speaking to each other in soft murmurs. They were lounging on multicolored pillows set on a patchwork of carpets that covered the sand.

Katook felt his tail twitch with excitement as he slid off Quigga's back and tried to take in all the marvels before him. There were silver vessels filled with fruit, and dancers wearing veils and clicking castanets, and musicians who sat on a thick, fat cushion, playing stringed instruments and drums. Behind the musicians, sitting on an even bigger, fatter cushion, was a group of Patah, wearing huge, round turbans.

Glancing around at the reclining antelopes and Patah, Katook realized that most of them were gazing expectantly at the turbaned monkeys.

It's as though everyone is waiting for something about to begin, he thought.

Confused, he turned to Hasara. "What are they looking at?"

"Hush, now, come, there's some room over there."

Gingerly they picked their way through the audience, Quigga being particularly careful not to step on anyone with his hooves. A Patah in a long, flowing headdress offered them their choice of seats. Quigga settled on his knees on a wide silk-covered pillow, and Katook perched on a tall cushion in order to see over the heads of the Patah.

At the sound of a low whistle, everyone fell silent. And as if by one breath, the flames on all the candles and oil lamps went out.

From out of the darkness came a high, shrill voice. It was impossible to tell whether it was male or female, but this is what it said: "We know it now as the Dead City, but it was once called Geebah: the fire inside the flame. The outer walls were covered in gold, and the buildings were richly studded with precious gems. And the gold and jewels of Geebah burned so brilliantly in the sun that the city could be seen glowing from one horizon to the other."

The musicians began to play a quiet, almost eerie melody. Katook's eyes widened as the darkness was suddenly filled with light, and the silhouette of the city appeared before them—as if magically suspended in the air.

The storyteller continued: "Although it is true that Geebah is dead now, it was not always so. Tonight we set our tents near the Dead City, and it calls on us to tell its story so that we may never forget.

"It is known that what made Geebah more precious than any city under the stars was not the gold or the jewels of the city, but its beloved ruler: King Hemeh. All who knew him gladly sang his praise. It was said that he was more giving than the sun and far more compassionate. His generosity was so great that he refused to drink until he knew

that no one was thirsty. He refused to eat until he knew that no one was hungry. He couldn't even sleep until all were sleeping.

"King Hemeh made peace with the desert. The winds never raged inside Geebah, and the water inside its golden walls was cool and honey-sweet." Katook's nostrils flared as a light honey scent filled the air inside the tent.

"Now, this king was blessed with two strong and handsome sons, and this comforted him greatly. He felt that as he grew old his beloved city, and all who lived there, would be loved by his sons as well as by himself. Many years passed, each as gentle as the one before

82

it, until finally the king knew that soon the wind would take his soul.

"Hemeh summoned his two sons to his deathbed and whispered his last words to them: 'Geebah is like a fire in the desert. And like a fire in a barren place with so little to feed it, it is a fragile thing. You two must tend this city carefully. Feed it with the generosity of your hearts and nurture it with your compassionate wisdom. Do this and you will find comfort and happiness here always.'

"But, of course, I would not be telling you this story if that was how things came to pass. Quite obviously, they did not. Upon King Hemeh's death, his two sons quarreled. They were not willing to share Geebah. They did not tend their magnificent city like a fragile fire. They did not feed it with their generosity or nurture it with compassionate wisdom. Instead, each tried to claim it as his own. And as we all know, when two fight over a single burning log, both end up getting burned. In time the brothers divided the city in two, and each brought in fierce, bone-crushing beasts to protect his half."

Katook felt Quigga stir with fear as the giant silhouette of a bone-crusher appeared before them. Katook glanced around nervously. None of the other animals seemed frightened. But he and Quigga shuddered together as magic and reality became as inseparable as music and song.

"The two brothers waged war," the storyteller continued. "Each tried to wrest control of Geebah from the other. The fighting raged on for years. Much of the city was destroyed and many lives were lost, but the brothers remained stubborn. Each refused to give in to the other. They called on dark magic, and each summoned spirits to join his armies. But these were evil spirits who could not be controlled, for they fed only on destruction. Thus the winds came."

At this, a wail of howling wind was heard, but the storyteller went on. "Winds so violent, they stripped the gold from the walls and ripped the gems from the buildings and scattered them through the desert. The water turned sour, and those who survived the battles were forced to flee their once beautiful city. It is said they escaped to the caves of the Beehive Pinnacles, and that their descendants are there to this day, dwelling with the dark spirits and delving even deeper into what is forbidden.

"The two brothers, however, stubbornly stayed behind with their bone-crushers, neither willing to surrender. That is how they grew old. And that is how they died. At last their bodies were eaten by the starving beasts, whose offspring, to this day, prowl the streets of this lifeless city, reminding us so that we may never forget Geebah's legacy of greed."

Suddenly someone let out a scream as a giant silhouette of one of the bone-crushers leapt out of the darkness and began to slowly prowl

85

the room. Katook watched its huge shape passing over the wide-eyed faces.

A loud growling and a baleful howl filled the tent. Katook felt a jolt of panic. The bone-crusher was pursued by even more fantastical monsters before it suddenly leapt straight up and vanished. There was a moment of stunned silence, then a great burst of light. An explosion of colored sparks filled the tent with a crackling chaos of color.

Again there was silence—for a long breath—then riotous paw-stomping and hooting erupted from every corner of the tent. But Katook, seeing the flecks of colored light, was reminded of Gamic's sacred magic, and threw himself onto his belly and pressed his forehead to the carpet. Nearby, Quigga had leapt to his feet and was trembling, as in a cold wind.

"What are you two doing?" asked a small Patah, perplexed.

"Nothing," said Quigga. "Stretching my legs. Is there anything wrong with that?"

"And him?" bleated an antelope fawn, nodding to Katook, who kept his eyes closed and his head down.

"I don't know," answered Quigga, as confused by Katook's posture as the fawn.

"What troubles you, Little One?" a grave voice intoned. It was Hasara, regarding him thoughtfully.

Katook looked up hesitantly and was surprised to see that the lamps were lit again, and he was the only one on his belly. "The priest's sacred fire . . . ," he began.

"The what?" asked Hasara.

"The colored light."

"You didn't think it was real, did you?" Hasara said. "It was part of the performance." Taking Katook gently by the paw, he led him toward the Patah who wore the giant round turbans. "These are our Masters of Illusion. It was their skill you saw."

The red-furred monkey who wore the most elaborate headdress gazed at Katook with shrewd eyes. "So we performed and you believed," he said softly.

Katook, unsure of what had happened, said nothing.

"Show him, Feluz," Hasara said.

"Watch carefully," Feluz told Katook. Then he tugged on an almost invisible thread hanging from the wall behind him. A large panel of pale silk dropped from the canopy ceiling and rippled lightly in the breeze.

Feluz nodded to one of the other turbaned Patah, and the fabric was lit from behind by a "magic lantern." This was a large box elaborately carved with the faces of animals, their mouths and eyes wide open. Inside the animals' eyes and mouths were glass lenses, lit from within by candles. Glass plates with images of the story painted on them were then slid into the magic lantern. The image on the first plate was the silhouette of Geebah that had begun the performance.

The smallest of the illusionists opened the stopper of a delicate glass vessel, and the scent of honey filled the air.

"And the bone-crushers and the other beasts?" Katook asked, not quite convinced. After all, they had leapt through the tent. They hadn't been images on a screen.

Feluz pulled another thread. This time a trapdoor in the canopy ceiling opened, and a huge, very realistic bone-crusher puppet dropped down and began bounding through the tent. One of the other illusionists pulled on another thread, and a second trapdoor opened, releasing a fantastical puppet.

Katook watched, amazed. They looked so real.

Quigga lifted his head. "Illusions. Of course."

But one thing still troubled Katook. "And the priest's sacred fire?" he asked.

Hasara offered his paw to Katook again. "Come. Let's go outside into the night glow and I'll show you."

Katook turned to Quigga to see if he'd join them.

"Don't look at me," Quigga replied. "If you'll remember, I wasn't the one who lounged around on a beautiful back, carried through a sandstorm and chased by beasts. I'm exhausted. If you want to wander around under the night glow, that's up to you."

Katook saw that the muscles in Quigga's legs were quivering and realized that he had had all the excitement he could handle.

"Of course," Katook said, understanding his friend. "Why don't you rest?"

Chapter Ten
THE MARKING

The sky was clear, and moonlight fell on Katook and Hasara as they stepped outside. It was quiet; most of the voices inside the camp were now still.

"Would you like me to show you the difference between magic and illusion?" asked Hasara.

"I think so," Katook answered hesitantly.

Hasara waved his arm across the starlit sky. "*That* is magic. While *this*"—he reached his paws into two different pouches slung over his shoulder—"is illusion." He tossed a handful of dust from each pouch into the air. The two clouds of dust mingled in the air then exploded in a burst of blue sparks that turned flame red before falling harmlessly onto the desert sand.

Katook leapt back, tail bristling, and was about to drop to his belly when Hasara gripped his elbow and held him upright.

"That was nothing more than two different types of ground stone reacting to each other."

Stunned, Katook wondered how many of Gamic's other "signs" from the Fossah were nothing more than dust and illusion.

"You must be weary, Small One," Hasara said. "But before you sleep, Ishan, our chieftain, desires to meet the strange visitor who made his bed in the Dead City."

He led Katook back inside the camp to a small chamber set off by hanging tapestries. "These are the quarters of our chieftain." At Katook's surprised expression he explained, "Though our camp doesn't approach the glory of ancient Geebah, our chieftain aspires to live with the same simplicity and generosity as King Hemeh. Go on in, he's waiting for you."

Katook looked nervously to Hasara, hoping that he'd join him, but his guide gestured for him to go in alone. Katook took a deep breath and entered. He found himself standing on a blue carpet in a simple room. There were cushions, carved wooden caskets, a low table with assorted silver vessels, several lit lampsticks, and two Patah, one large, one small, with their backs to him. They were sitting together on a chest. The larger of them turned. He was holding a dagger in one paw, a sword in the other. His cloak formed a train behind him. And his turban, while not as large as those of the illusionists, was still impressive. He motioned Katook forward.

"You must be Katook," he said. "I am Ishan, and this is my son, Healio. I was just teaching my son how to use his dagger to sharpen his sword." He set the weapons down on the chest and approached Katook. "Tell me, what led you to sleep with the bone-crushers, armed with nothing more than a needle-guide and an exhausted wind-drinker?" When Katook didn't answer, he barked, "Speak!"

"N-no, I mean, y-yes, Your Majesty," Katook finally stammered, not knowing what to call him.

"I am but the chieftain of the Patah. The only majesty we have here are the stars overhead."

"The rugs are very nice, too," said Katook, hoping that that was the right thing to say, and feeling his fur settle a bit.

Suddenly Healio trotted over to him and stood very close, staring and sniffing at his fur. "What's in there?" the chieftain's son demanded, pointing at the Kolloboo pouch that hung from Katook's neck.

Katook chose his words carefully. "Important things I need for my journey."

"Well, let's see these things, since they're so important," said Healio. Katook opened the pouch and carefully set the contents on the rug at his feet.

"Mmm," murmured Healio, fingering the objects. "Land-drawings and a needle-guide. We Patah have no need of those. But this . . . ahhh," he exclaimed, spying the seal. "What is this?"

"It's—" Katook began.

"I want it," said the chieftain's son, and started to grab it.

Instinctively, Katook snatched the precious seal and held it firmly in his paw. "I can't—"

"Give it to me!" Healio demanded shrilly.

"But I . . . you don't understand," stammered Katook, reluctant to give away the one thing he needed to find his kin.

Ishan's angry voice boomed as he commanded, "Healio, outside!"

Cringing, Healio quickly obeyed his father and scurried out of the tent, leaving Katook alone with Ishan, who snatched his swords from the bench. His eyes blazing with fury, he rose to his hind legs and strode toward Katook. The curved blades blinked yellow in the candlelight, then turned black as Ishan turned them over in his paws.

Katook began to tremble. His tail bristled. He wanted to run, to hide. But he just crouched there, silent and terrified.

Finally Ishan spoke in a voice both low and cold. "Come here." Katook slowly crept forward.

"I've done something wrong. Please tell me what it is," he begged.

"Look away!" demanded Ishan as he slowly circled the young lemur. "We saved you from the bone-crushers and welcomed you into our camp, and yet you deny my son's simple request."

Puzzled by the chief's anger, Katook gripped the seal meant for Nadab. "This . . . ? But I didn't mean—"

"Silence!" Then Ishan's voice became dangerously quiet. "Perhaps you slept during the story told this very evening. Perhaps it wasn't made clear to you that we of the desert have no choice but to share everything we own with each other. It's either that or die." He was standing on a wooden chest. "Did you come here to die, tree-creature?"

Katook crouched even lower. "N-n-no, sir," he managed to stutter, his mouth so dry he could barely move his tongue. "I'll gladly give you anything I have, but if I give away my seal, I give away my only chance of finding others like me."

"Others like you," said the chieftain with disgust. "Then what am I?"

"You?" Katook asked.

"Are you and I so different that you must feel so alone?"

"But I'm from another place. I look so—"

"So different?" interrupted Ishan, finishing Katook's thought. "When the stars look down at us, do we appear so different to them? And when we thirst, is our thirst different? Our hunger? Or maybe it's when we celebrate a great joy. Perhaps our happiness is different? Is that what you're trying to say?"

Ashamed and confused, Katook stared down at the rug he knelt on. Woven into the fabric were yellow stars in a swirling sea of cobalt blue. He felt as if he were no longer in his body, but had somehow fallen into a small but very shiny azure star in the rug. He felt himself moving, slowly swirling in the indigo sky. And then he heard a very faint voice. "Listen," it said. It sounded as if it were coming from someplace very far away. "The words are true."

Katook looked up at Ishan. The distant voice hadn't come from him because the chieftain was staring at him, waiting for his answer.

"How are you and I so different that you feel so alone?" demanded Ishan.

Katook touched the seal. *I've lost my family and my home,* he thought.

If I give away this seal, I lose Nadab, the only one I know who can help me find others like me.

Katook clutched the tiny seal, then slowly, hesitantly, he opened his paw and offered Ishan the gift the Kolloboo had given him. "We're not so different," he admitted quietly. "Here . . . please, tell your son that I'm sorry and give this to him."

The chieftain took the seal but handed it back to Katook without even glancing at it. "Keep it. I want something else."

Katook blinked in confusion. "I have a needle-guide and a map," he offered. "But Hasara showed me how you use the stars to find direction. So you may not have any use for them."

"I don't want your needle-guide or your land-drawing," said Ishan as he turned his two swords over and over in his paws.

"Then what?"

"This," Ishan yowled, leaping into the air. His swords flashed—and cut a bloody nick in Katook's ear.

Katook yelped. His ear stung and he felt himself bleeding, yet he knew he wasn't seriously hurt.

"That's to remind you that from this day forward you must never again act as if you're alone. You may go now." Ishan sheathed his swords and turned away.

Katook returned to the main area of the tent, where he found Quigga fast asleep among the antelopes. The sight comforted Katook.

Quigga opened one eye and said, "Are you all right?"

"Go back to sleep. I'm fine." And Katook realized that, in fact, he was fine, and happy to have a friend like Quigga to curl up with.

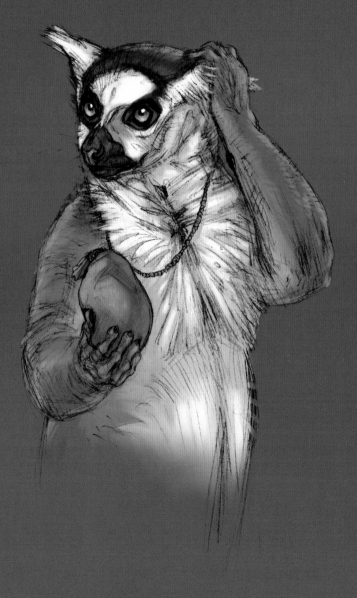

At dawn, Katook woke to find the Patah camp packing up. He and Quigga watched as carpets were rolled, and silver vessels and musical instruments were tucked into chests. Cushions were stacked and tied in great canvas bundles, which were then tied onto the sides of the glyptodonts. And a number of the Patah stood on the backs of the glyptodonts, carefully folding up the great golden canopy.

A shrill, trilling cry of alarm pierced the peaceful camp as two mounted Patah scouts raced toward it.

Katook saw Hasara's paw tighten on his sword. "To the glyptodonts!" he shouted. "Warriors to your mounts!"

The Patah camp was now raging with activity. Young and old, male and female rushed about, abandoning all preparations. Pots and chests tumbled everywhere. The females, children, and old ones scrambled for the safety of the circle that the glyptodonts were re-forming.

Katook and Quigga followed the warriors out beyond the protective circle. Every warrior held a sword, and every gaze was fixed on the distance.

"What are they looking at?" Katook asked Quigga, who was stamping and shifting impatiently. All Katook saw was that the sky was a bruised gray, the sun still hanging just below the horizon.

"That," said Quigga, his voice tight with fear. "Get on my back. Now!"

Katook scrambled up. Following the quagga's gaze, he saw an enormous, dark dust cloud moving quickly over the dunes. Another sandstorm? Looking more carefully at the cloud, Katook realized it was actually a flock of enormous, long-legged birds. Their heads were as large as Quigga's, and they had savage, cruelly hooked beaks. They weren't flying but running toward the Patah camp. Katook was able to pick out twenty, maybe thirty of them, their tiny black wings beating uselessly at their sides.

"What are they?"

"Phorcus," Quigga answered, his eyes darting around for a way out. But all around them there was a commotion of voices raised in battle cries and the metal clang of swords being drawn and sharpened.

"We have to get out of here!" Quigga cried. But his voice was drowned out by a vicious screeching as the birds attacked in a dark chaos of talons and beaks and furiously flapping wings.

95

The glyptodonts whirled their spiked tails in the air, defending the Patah within the inner circle, but the phorcus were quick. One instant Katook had one coming toward him; the next it was screaming past, a dead warrior caught in its beak.

The Patah fought bravely. A number of warriors rode the glyptodonts, brandishing swords, bows, and javelins. The rest were mounted on spear-horned antelopes, darting in and out, spattered with blood and feathers. But the phorcus attacked in waves. One of the antelopes stumbled, tossing its rider into a gaping maw. The terrible sound of screams and screeches was deafening.

With the wild eyes of a stallion protecting his herd, Quigga charged into the fray, biting and rearing. Katook held on tight to his mane, barely able to believe that his friend was fighting so fiercely. Quigga kicked and shattered a phorcu jaw, and then another. His hooves slashed, and one of the birds' shins snapped. He bit, and a phorcu's throat was torn out. Suddenly one of the phorcus slammed against him, and he fell backward to the sand, throwing off Katook before scrambling to his feet.

"Get back on!" Quigga screamed at Katook. "Get on, *now*!"

At that moment a Patah sword whizzed right past Katook's head and sank deep into one of the birds, dropping it instantly.

"Get on!"

"Wait!" cried Katook. "I want to help, too!" He dashed to the dead carcass and tried to yank the great sword from its breast. But the sword was far too heavy and stuck too deep.

Quigga rushed forward and grabbed Katook by the scruff of his neck. In an instant, the sword was torn loose from the bird. Katook almost dropped it, then grabbed hold of it with all his strength. Although he knew he wasn't strong enough to wield it, he held on to it, shoulders aching as he dangled from Quigga's mouth. And then through the confusion and the dust, Katook saw Ishan.

The Patah chieftain lay on the ground, one leg bleeding and useless, his sword broken beside him. A huge phorcu stood over him, about to strike.

Ears flattened, Quigga bore down on them, and Katook knew what he must do. "Ishan! Here!" With all his small strength, he tossed him the sword as Quigga raced past. Katook saw the chieftain catch the sword with a paw. Then a lightning slash—and the phorcu crumbled in a heap.

With one backsweep of his neck, Quigga tossed Katook onto his back and doubled back at a gallop to Ishan.

"Wind-drinker . . . small Katook!" shouted Ishan as they approached. "My life is in debt to you. But this battle is not yours, nor is it for you. Now go!"

"But—" panted Katook.

"You must go!" cried Ishan, gesturing away from the battle. "Do not disobey me!"

Quigga galloped faster and faster across the sands, racing away from the sounds of battle and eastward into the vast open desert, where the dunes gave way to rockier ground.

Katook heard it before he saw it: pounding footfalls followed by a bloodcurdling screech. A bloody beak gnashed at his head, just missing him. He glanced back, horrified. At least a dozen phorcus were chasing them.

Quigga galloped harder. Katook clung desperately. The phorcus closed for another strike. This time a beak tore at Quigga, leaving three bloody slashes across his flanks.

"Quigga!" Katook cried.

But Quigga ignored the pain and ran harder.

Another phorcu hurtled toward them, its hooked beak aimed at Quigga's head. Quigga cut hard on the sand and the bird's beak missed its target, its stubby wing hitting Katook full in the face. Katook felt his muscles lock with fear. If he hadn't managed to grab Quigga's mane and pull himself back up, the blow would have knocked him to the ground, where he would have been easy prey.

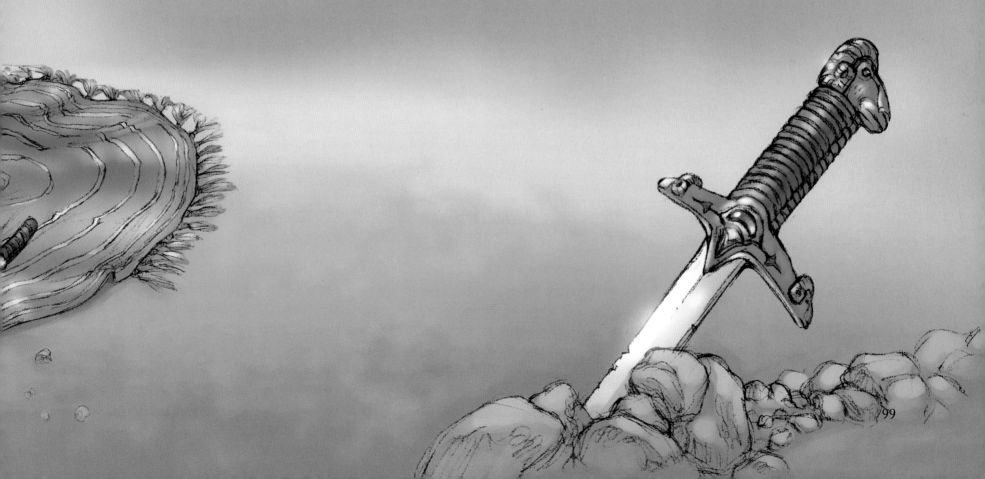

99

Quigga raced grimly, his eyes ringed with white as the huge carnivorous birds bore down on them. Katook gripped Quigga's neck fiercely and buried his face in his sweaty mane. He tasted blood and wondered if it was Quigga's or his own. *It doesn't matter,* Katook thought. *It's only a matter of time before these creatures tear us both to pieces.*

The bone-rattling pounding suddenly stopped. The horrible sound of the screeching birds faded away. And the air turned cool. Flying . . . they were . . . flying . . .

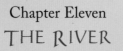

Chapter Eleven
THE RIVER

Katook opened his eyes, looked down past Quigga's shoulder, and saw nothing. The desert beneath Quigga's hooves had vanished. Far below him, he saw distant rocks, plumes of spray, and what looked like a river. *It is a river,* Katook realized, *and we're falling straight toward it!*

Splash and under! Katook held fast to Quigga's powerful shoulders as they broke the surface and were instantly dragged downstream.

Quigga fought the current as he tried to swim toward the shore, but every time he got within a couple of lengths of the curving bank, he was yanked back into the middle of the whitecapped river.

Sitting high on Quigga's shoulders, Katook could hear what Quigga couldn't, and the sound terrified him. He'd heard it once before back on Bo-hibba. It was the crushing, thunderous sound of a waterfall. But the sound of *this* waterfall was much louder than the one he remembered . . .

It's not far off, Katook reasoned. *It must be just around one of these bends.*

Katook felt the fight in Quigga's desperately churning legs growing weaker. The river was winning. Katook sensed that it wouldn't be long before Quigga gave in to the pull of the water and they both drowned.

Katook leaned all the way forward, close to Quigga's soft cheeks. He could see Quigga's nostrils frantically flaring and contracting.

"You're strong!" Katook screamed over the roaring water. "You can do this!"

Just then a wave swept over them and pushed them underwater. Katook's lungs burned for air, but he fought his panic and held on tight to Quigga. Finally he saw a flash of blue sky as they burst through the surface—only to be swept under by another wave.

"I'm sorry," hacked Quigga. "I'm so tired—"

Katook sensed that if they went under again, it would be for the last time.

"Without me clinging to your neck you can make it," Katook yelled. "I'll—"

"No," coughed Quigga. "Stay with me. You don't weigh—"

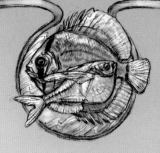

Then a still, quiet voice, strangely clear above the rushing water, spoke to Katook from someplace inside him. *"Don't let go, Little One. Don't let go."*

So Katook stayed with his friend. *At least neither of us will die alone,* he thought.

Up ahead, the river took one last sharp turn that was piled high with broken trees and tumbled-smooth boulders. Then it opened onto a wide plain of cold, swift water that suddenly disappeared into the horizon.

Katook and Quigga shot into the hairpin turn and into a mass of branches jammed between two huge boulders. They gulped air. Then the jam gave way.

Katook screamed as they shot out into a swirling eddy and hurtled toward the waterfall.

Quigga's head strained above the whitecaps, and Katook caught the horrible glimpse of nothing between them and the horizon. No sharp turns. No boulders. No logs. He knew what was coming: a straight drop. He shut his eyes again, sure that it would be for the last time. Then he felt Quigga rising beneath him.

Katook opened his eyes and saw that they were being supported by not one, but *three* long, smooth, pale pink river dolphins! Amazed, Katook tightened his grip on Quigga's wet mane as the dolphins swam them back upstream, propelling themselves against the current with powerful whips of their tails.

The dolphins carried them around an outcropping of boulders and into the shelter of a small, shallow pool at the river's edge. Once safely inside the calm inlet, the dolphins gently eased their passengers off their backs. Quigga let out a deep, wheezing sigh. With Katook barely conscious, clinging to his mane, he slogged through the water, picking his way over rocks and roots until he stood on uncertain legs on the muddy bank of the river.

Katook lay flat behind the curve of Quigga's withers, coughing up water.

"That's right, furry one," called one of the river dolphins in a high-pitched voice. "Give back some of that water you've taken from my home. But your friend, the large one"—he indicated Quigga with his snout—"he is wounded badly. Watch out for him." And with that the dolphins slipped back into the river's depths and vanished.

Katook forgot his own weary, wet discomfort. He slipped off Quigga's back and Quigga turned away from him, moving slowly toward the shore. That's when Katook saw the bloody gashes where the phorcus had ripped into Quigga's back and the patches of raw pink flesh where the river's rocks had torn his beautiful hide.

"Quigga, stop," Katook said.

The wounded quagga stumbled over the twisted mangrove roots that wove their way through the black mud. Shivering with pain and shock, he slogged through murky water thick with water lilies. It wasn't until he was past a large boulder, and finally out of sight of the river, that he slowly collapsed to the ground.

He lay on his side, his chest heaving with each breath. His eyes were half shut, and his mouth hung open.

Katook crouched beside him and gently smoothed his mane, making sure every hair was perfectly in place, exactly the way he liked it. "Rest, Quigga. Dream of running with your herd." He watched as Quigga's long blond eyelashes fell across his eyes as slowly as a summer cloud drifting across the sun. "Sleep," Katook whispered.

Katook sat there a long time until his friend slept. Then Katook looked up at the large boulder that separated the stream from the banyan tree sheltering Quigga. Thinking the boulder might make a good lookout, Katook scrambled to its top. From there, he looked across the river, oily black and swift. *There's no way we'll get back across,* he realized. *There's no way we'll ever see the Patah again. And if I can't find them, how will I ever get back on the path to Nadab?*

He reached for his map and needle-guide. But to his horror both were gone, stolen from him by the river. Miraculously, the little clay seal was still there. Then it struck Katook just how pointless it was to have the key to unlock a door when he had no idea of how to find that door.

Katook sat there, wondering what they were going to do. He was certain of only one thing. *There's always some way out of every place. I just have to find it.* That's when he heard the sound of a rattle. It was shivering very quickly. And behind the sound of this rattle someone, or something, was humming.

Katook turned, looked back toward the noise, and saw a huddle of orange-furred monkeys hunched over Quigga. Katook stiffened with fear. Quigga lay motionless on the ground. The monkeys were all wearing colorful feathered headdresses, and the largest of them waved a hollow rattle back and forth across the length of Quigga's body. Then Katook relaxed a bit as he realized that several other monkeys were gently treating Quigga's wounds with herbs, poultices, and salves.

Katook scrambled off the boulder and approached them, curious but also wary.

Without turning, the large monkey with the rattle spoke in a surprising voice, deep as thunder. "Don't worry, your friend is in good hands. You trust this, yes?"

"Yes," Katook replied before he had time to think about it. "I do."

"Yes, good," said the monkey. He stopped shaking the rattle, then slowly turned to gaze at Katook. "My name is Dikemba. We are the Boskiis."

What first struck Katook as the monkey turned to face him was not the kindness in his small, almond-shaped eyes, or the brilliance of his feathered headdress, but his nose. It was huge. In fact, it was so big it looked like a soft bag had settled in the center of his face. And when he blinked, which he did often, he did it slowly, as if he enjoyed it.

Katook's nostrils quivered as a terrible stink filled the air. He couldn't tell whether it came from Quigga or the Boskiis who were treating him. "What are you doing to my friend?" he asked.

Dikemba tilted his head to one side and answered, "We are leading him back to where he once was."

"But that smell—what are you putting on him?"

"Flowers and herbs from the Seeleebee Traders, mixed with our own wishes and songs, all to bring your friend whole again."

"Will he be all right?" asked Katook softly.

Dikemba touched Quigga's rising and falling chest. "Your friend's wounds are festering. He burns and shivers with fever, but I believe it will pass."

"Of course he'll be all right," said a tiny voice from someplace close by. A small mouse deer rose up from behind Quigga's haunches and stood self-importantly at his side.

"This is Sia," explained Dikemba. "Apparently upon first sight of your friend, she felt a certain kinship. The two of them being—"

"—handsome and noble creatures," Sia jumped in.

The little mouse deer had two sharp, fanglike tusks that would have made her appear fierce if she had been much, much bigger. But Katook could tell by the proud way she stood that

Sia considered herself a powerful creature.

"I am currently braiding your friend's tail," Sia continued. "Do you know if he prefers a three- or four-strand braid?"

"I really don't know. We never talked about it."

"I shall give him a four-strand." Katook's eyes widened as Sia pointed with a delicate hoof, directing a young Boskii in the proper method of braiding.

As the day wore on, the Boskiis continued tending to Quigga's wounds. Together they sang songs to Quigga and blended flowers into colored pastes, which they gently applied to the gashes on his haunches. Quigga's fever dreams seemed to lessen. His legs lay still. His breathing became soft and even.

Sitting close to Quigga's side, Katook was dozing off when he heard a whisper: "How do I look?" Quigga's eyes were half open. "Do I look fetching?"

Katook smiled and gently touched the soft round of Quigga's cheek. "You look like a hero, magnificent, as always."

"As I should," Quigga answered weakly. Then his eyes closed again.

"Come," said Dikemba. "He will sleep now and find himself again. He will be well."

"But I should stay by his side," Katook said with concern.

"No need for that," said Sia grandly. "I will watch over him." And with that she ferociously bared her tiny tusks.

Doing his best not to laugh, Katook bowed to the bold little deer. "Will you watch over me, too?"

"You have my word."

"Very well, then," said Dikemba. "Let us get off this ground and into the trees before night falls. We'll return when our dreams pass."

While Quigga shivered all through the night with his fever dreams, Katook and Sia stayed by his side. The Boskiis, their healing done for the day, disappeared into their homes high in the banyan trees. In the morning Katook looked up at the sound of Dikemba and the other Boskiis descending from the trees. Katook marveled as their headdresses caught rays of early-morning light, making the sheer blades of the feathers glow brightly in a rainbow of color.

"How is our patient feeling today?" asked Dikemba.

Quigga lifted his head. His fever gone and his mind now alert, he saw the Boskiis clearly for the first time. He squinted, as if in disbelief, as the baggy-nosed creatures slowly moved toward them.

"Katook," he whispered, "I have seen some ugly animals in my travels—"

"Shhh . . . ," whispered Katook.

"I mean, *ugly* animals," Quigga went on. "In fact, recently I've been attacked by snarling, drooling beasts and clawed by hideous carnivorous birds, but these are, undoubtedly, the ugliest creatures I have ever seen in my life."

"Quigga! They saved your life!" Katook said in an urgent undertone as Dikemba and the other Boskiis approached.

"Well, I don't remember anything about that, but will you look at their noses?" Quigga continued, oblivious to the fact that they were all staring at him.

"Our noses?" repeated Dikemba, flaring his nostrils slightly. "I can't speak for anyone else's nose, but I can say that mine is being tortured at this very moment."

"Tortured?" asked Katook.

"With each and every inhalation," the leader went on. Then he turned his gaze on Quigga and continued, "My poor *large* nose is suffering under the horrid odor of a sickly-sweet plains-runner."

Quigga got to his feet and stood there quivering indignantly.

"I think he means you," Katook explained to Quigga in a whisper.

"I know who he's talking to!" said Quigga, outraged. "He thinks I smell!"

"Horridly," agreed the Boskii leader, who pinched his very ample nose between his big toe and fore toe. "But before we address your hygiene, or lack of it, as the case may be, let me first say that I am happy to see that you are feeling better. My name is Dikemba. And you are?"

Quigga threw back his head, looked down on Dikemba disdainfully, then began: "I am Quigga. Son of Quilla, son Quiloz, son of Quiggoo—"

"Of course. But we will call you Snogii."

"You'll call me what?" said Quigga in horror.

"Snogii, the one who is smelled before he is seen."

Quigga yelled after Dikemba, "Maybe I should call you Nosey or Creature with the Giant Prune Stuck on His Face . . ."

Dikemba turned to Katook, "I am not certain if it is a good thing or a bad thing," he began with a smile, "but it seems your friend has found himself again. Perhaps now you'll come and meet the rest of us?"

Katook gazed up at the trees. They were unlike anything he had ever seen. Then he realized that it was actually only one great tree with trunks growing from its branches and branches growing from its trunks. They formed a maze of arches and open pavilions rising out of the forest floor. High above, connected lodges of various sizes, woven of leaf, branch, twig, and vine, were secured in the branches. They reminded Katook of his own lost home, far away on Bo-hibba. Some of the structures were very large indeed and could accommodate many monkeys. All had high, peaked roofs, with sharp spikes that jutted outward.

All at once there were dark shapes on the wet branches, Boskiis scurrying everywhere. Katook could see their eyes, glistening like raindrops among the leaves.

"*He will come to you,*" sang Dikemba. "*So hurry, make your lodge warm for him.*"

As if swept away by a strong wind, the Boskiis vanished.

Katook looked up at Dikemba and asked, "Who will come to them?"

"Why, you, of course." And with that, Dikemba and the rest of the Boskiis disappeared into the wet, dark green foliage overhead.

Katook hung back, afraid to leave his friend alone on the jungle floor.

"Oh, go ahead," said Quigga grumpily. "My little friend and I"—he nodded in Sia's direction—"will entertain ourselves down here on this sodden mess of earth and pray that we both don't get hoof-rot."

Trailing the Boskiis, Katook pulled himself up into the thickly limbed banyan tree. Moving smoothly from branch to branch, he felt his muscles warm and stretch as he climbed. For him this was home, or at least something close to it. After the ocean, and the danger in Acco, and the strangeness in Kolloboo, and the barren emptiness of the desert, it felt wonderful to have the comfort of trees overhead and the sweet smell of fruit in the air. The rain forest was like an old friend suddenly found again.

Katook reached an opening in the layers of branches and from there was able to look out across the canopy of trees. To the west, beyond the river, in the direction from which they'd come, he could see the dun crags of the desert bluffs. And in the other three directions, as far as he could see, was a vast steaming emerald bowl of jungle, the eastern border lost in a blue-gray mist.

It began to rain. Plump drops seemed to push from the sky, as if in a hurry to disappear into the deep loam that covered the forest floor. And when it didn't seem possible for the rain to fall any harder, it did. Rain so thick it was impossible to see more than an arm's-length away.

On a branch above him, Dikemba tilted his head back. Ignoring the rain that splashed fat and heavy on his face, he began to sing to the trees. It was a long, low song that sounded like an owl praising the moon.

"This way!" Katook heard from above. He looked up and saw one of the Boskiis waving him into the largest of their dwellings.

The structure was much cruder than the tightly woven basket homes Katook was used to, and far more colorful. The outside was plastered with leaves of different types and sizes, and the wooden door was decorated with brightly colored feathers.

Dikemba waited for Katook just inside the entrance. He poked his ample nose out through the feathers and smiled. "It's warm and dry inside, come."

Katook looked down through the falling rain, hoping to see Quigga.

"Your friend has found shelter under the tree," said Dikemba, as if reading Katook's thoughts. "You needn't worry. He'll be comfortable there."

"I wish he could climb."

"And he probably wishes you could carry him on your back. Each to our nature."

Katook smiled at this, knowing it was true.

"He'll be safe. We sang to the Great Ones and asked them to watch over your friend. Now, come, it's warm inside."

And before Katook had a chance to ask who the Great Ones were, or how they would watch over Quigga, Dikemba ducked through the doorway.

The Boskii lodge was indeed warm and cozy. Someone was playing a flute, someone else a bowed instrument, their music accompanied by the rain that danced on the thatched roof. The elders were smoking long, slender pipes. Others were eating and talking. It had been such a long time since Katook had felt the comfort of warm bodies huddled all around him. Even though it wasn't the same as being with his own family, it was wonderful nonetheless.

It seemed every Boskii in the lodge had a question for Katook.

"What do you dream?" a young one called out.

"Pardon me?" said Katook.

"Your dreams," said another. "What are they made of?"

"I don't understand. They are made of dreams."

A Boskii with a single feather stuck in his headdress murmured "Amazing" as he moved very close to Katook and stared intently at him.

He's staring into my eyes, thought Katook. *He sees the curse that's been put on me.*

"Is it my eyes?" Katook asked timidly, afraid of the answer he might receive.

"Yes, but not the blue eyes looking at me," explained the Boskii, crouching in front of him. "The eyes that see in your sleep. Your dream eyes."

Dikemba combed his fingers through his headdress, making it whistle like wind in the trees; then he spoke. "Our friend's dream eyes are cloudy. We shall sleep so that we can dream them becoming clear again."

"*Oooma,*" they all sang together in one long, sweet, and sleepy note.

"*Oooma,*" whispered Dikemba in response.

Everyone found their place in the lodge and prepared to sleep. Worn out, and confused, Katook curled up and closed his eyes. *My dream eyes,* he thought. Then he lay there thinking how long

it had been since he could remember one of his dreams. *A long time ago,* he thought, *another lifetime ago.*

All around him he could hear the Boskiis stretching, curling, unwinding into sleep. He felt so happy, because what he had missed most, even more than the yummy warmth of being cuddled by furry bodies all around him, was the sound of breathing. Soft, easy, effortless. The breath of sleep. The breath of dreams.

Soon he felt his own breath slow and begin to join the rhythm of those around him—the rise and fall of their bellies almost singing to him, urging him to merge with them. And he would have given himself to their collective sleepy breath willingly if it wasn't for the picture that popped into his head of his poor, wet friend, far from his herd in a jungle that frightened him, standing all alone in the pouring rain.

At last Katook's concern for Quigga overpowered any chance he had at finding sleep. He untangled himself from the sleeping Boskiis, being careful not to interrupt the music of their slumber, and slipped outside.

He climbed down the tree and found Quigga standing beneath the arch of a banyan branch, with Sia standing under him. Quigga looked even more pathetic than Katook had remembered. His head hung low as he stared at the ground with the saddest expression Katook had ever seen. He turned his woeful eyes toward Katook.

"I couldn't sleep," Katook said over the beating rain. "Would you mind terribly if I shared your—"

"—my castle?" finished Quigga with a faint smile.

"Yes, your castle."

"I hate this place, Katook."

"I know."

"It's dank and dark and filled with trees. It oppresses me. It closes me in. It's a *devourer.* A prison, I tell you.

What else can you call a place if you can't run freely, the wind in your mane? Where you can't spy a predator before it springs? What kind of place is this?"

"Actually, it's a lot like where I used to live," said Katook.

"Then you should be happy they made you leave such a miserable place," said Quigga irritably. But Katook could see that he didn't feel good about saying it.

"You two sleep," said Sia. "I'll stay up and protect you."

And with that, the little mouse deer bared her tiny fangs and growled. It sounded more like a purr than a growl, but the intention was clear and both Katook and Quigga struggled not to laugh.

Quigga found a dry spot and lowered himself to the ground. Katook nuzzled against his friend's cheek and settled between his forelegs, listening to Quigga's great heart above him, a steady drum playing softly to the music of the rain.

Chapter Thirteen
SWEETER THAN HONEY

Katook woke with a yawn and a stretch. The rain had stopped. Sunlight was filtering through the thick canopy of branches. A low fog of warm steam rose from the forest floor and hung so thickly, it seemed as if every drop of rain that had fallen was trying to find its way back into the sky so it could fall again. And hanging in this moist air was the sound of animals: the chirping, grunting, buzzing, hissing sound of creatures greeting the return of the sun with their finest voice.

Katook turned to Quigga but found him still blissfully asleep, his legs folded and Sia curled up beside him.

Looking up, Katook expected to see the Boskiis lounging in the sun, but instead he saw them climbing the massive banyan tree. He watched them make their way past the lodge they had slept in, then out of sight, their round golden bottoms disappearing into the foliage.

"Follow us," one of them called down to Katook. "Hurry, it is your time."

"My time?"

The Boskii kept climbing Then Katook heard, over—or just under—the buzz, hum, and hiss of the rain forest, the sound of drums. He stole another look at his sleeping friend then quickly scrambled up into the tree. He couldn't tell where the sound was coming from. All he knew was that it came from above. The rain forest was so dense that all he could see were leaves and tree limbs and more leaves. He hurried toward the drumming, as if drawn to it, leaping from branch to branch, always climbing higher.

It had been a long time since Katook had traveled through trees like this, and his heart seemed to open wider and wider as he flew. The sense of his paws gripping and releasing and the muscles in his arms and legs stretching and growing warm with exertion felt wonderful after the long night on the wet ground below.

The drumming grew louder as Katook made his way up into the tree, past the lodge, higher and higher until the leaves thinned out and the banyan trunk grew narrow. Suddenly he stopped. Above him, suspended by a web of green vines, was a building. Well, not really a building, more a primitive tangle of branches, large and small, straight and twisted, that had been woven together into what looked like a giant, upside-down bird's nest. Flame-red flowers grew from its sides, and these flowers were slowly swaying and opening and closing, as if they were breathing. Each time the flowers exhaled, they released tiny puffs of lemon-yellow pollen that hung heavy in the mist.

And from inside the tangled branches came music. It sounded like drums of all sizes, tens of them, playing all at once. The rhythm rose and fell, then abruptly became silent before rising again. Beneath the drumming, Katook heard another sound—a low, peaceful hum that he could feel vibrating up and out of the hut and through the trees.

Katook breathed in the sweet puffs of pollen that floated up into the warm air, then lay back on a branch. He had raced to get up here, but now he felt as if he had all the time in the world. He was dozing off when he heard: "It is your time."

Groggy, Katook looked up and saw Dikemba leaning out from the twig structure. The Boskii shaman blinked twice then disappeared back into the nest.

Katook slowly climbed the last few branches until he was even with an oddly shaped opening in the side of the structure. *This must be the entrance,* he realized, though from where he stood he couldn't see inside. Katook felt his every sense alert. His nose twitched, trying to identify a familiar scent. His fur was raised, gauging temperature and the subtlest changes in the air. All he could tell was that there was something in the hut different from anything he'd ever encountered— and it was much stronger than he was. And yet he wasn't frightened. In fact, Katook felt called by the presence inside to enter. He moved toward the strange structure.

The drumming stopped the instant Katook entered. He slowly turned in place. The Boskiis sat serenely in a wide circle, their backs to the wall of the hut, their paws still on the drums they held between their legs. The center of the round nest was open to the blue sky in a small circle, like a pupil staring out of a very large eye. Standing under the roofless center of the hut, flooded in a fat beam of light, was Dikemba, his feathered headdress waving in a light breeze.

The Boskii leader was surrounded by an inner circle of Boskiis who were blowing stout, hollow branches. The musicians inhaled together but took turns exhaling, creating a low, layered, breathy music.

As Katook listened, a strange thing began to happen to him—he felt his heart and the rhythm of the music beat together. It was as if the musicians were matching the rhythm of his heartbeat, or his heart was beating in rhythm with their music. He couldn't tell which.

Dikemba's slowly blinking eyes were fixed on him, and the Boskii leader was motioning him toward the center of the hut. "Stand in the sunlight," said Dikemba with a faraway voice. "Yes, right here in the very center."

Dikemba stepped aside, revealing a low stone table. Resting on it was a small glass jar filled with glowing amber liquid.

"You came to us, and we to you,"
Dikemba continued. "The Creator calls.
Now you can listen to the music of
dream-visions, and we will listen, too."

Katook wondered why he was
talking so peculiarly.

Dikemba gently placed his paw on Katook's forehead.

"Dream with me. Close your eyes."

Katook did as he was told. The hollow-branch
musicians hushed their music to a whisper. Katook felt
his heartbeat slow way down. And he felt the warm sun on his fur.
His feet seemed to have grown roots, and the roots fell through the
banyan and into the earth far below. He felt his neck stretching
upward, his head tilting back, his face yearning for the sky above.

"You were sent away," he heard Dikemba say.
Katook felt his chest tighten, but he remained
silent, his eyes closed.

"You were sent away because you were cursed."

"Yes," said Katook very softly, though Dikemba
wasn't asking for an answer; he was merely stating
a fact.

"You were told you went where you should not have gone. That you
saw what you should not have seen. And that who you are is not who
you should be."

Tears filled Katook's eyes. "It's true," he admitted, his voice a
hoarse whisper.

"No. What they call true is not *the* Truth. Listen to the song
of your dreams, Katook. . . . Listen."

Katook felt the music of the hollow branches rise then fall, and with it his heartbeat, as if the music were somehow inside him. Tears slid down the fur on his cheeks. They weren't tears of sadness, but of something he had no name for.

Dikemba pressed his paw into Katook's forehead and continued. "Do you hear it? It is the still, small voice that is always with you. It is the voice that is at the heart of the world."

Katook opened his eyes and stared up at Dikemba. "But look at me. Look at my eyes! I'm cursed."

Dikemba gazed fully into his blue eyes. "And then am I cursed looking into them?"

"Yes," answered Katook, filled with shame. "And now I'm afraid that *all* of you are in danger." Finally, he'd admitted what he'd felt all along but had been afraid to say aloud: Disaster followed him. After all, look at what had happened in Acco and to the Patah. Look at all the horrible things that had happened to Quigga ever since they'd become friends.

"Listen to me, Katook. You might doubt that what I tell you is true, just as you may doubt what you know is true—but will you listen?"

"I'll try." He felt so strange, as if he could no longer be certain of anything.

"Your blue eyes are neither a curse nor an accident. It is even possible that they are a blessing. You've been singled out. There's a reason. But I must tell you, Blue-Eyed One, that what you will see on the journey ahead of you is not going to be easy for you. It will not be easy for you at all."

"But my journey is over. I'm lost. I have no needle-guide, no map, no stars to see. How am I ever supposed to find Nadab in the land of the Golden Monkeys and find my kin?"

"Direction?" said Dikemba with a smile. "Is that all you're looking for?"

Dikemba carefully lifted the jar from the table, peeled away its wax seal, and dipped four fingers into it, coating each of them with the gooey golden fluid. "Now close your eyes, and keep them closed until I tell you to open them."

Katook did as he was told, and Dikemba began to sing softly, dabbing one finger at a time on Katook's face, his forehead first, then his chin, his right cheek and left.

This is what Dikemba sang:

To the North, South, East, and West,
From the Crocodile's Bed to the Eagle's Nest,
From the bud to the bloom to the restless bee,
Watch, hear, wait, and see!

120

Katook felt a drop of the amber liquid slip down his forehead and into his mouth. Curious, he tasted it. It was deliciously sweet, and he realized it was honey. He stood there rapt, caught in the sunlight, the taste of the honey, and the slow, soft piping of music and birds. With his eyes closed, Katook didn't see the brilliant blue butterfly flutter down through the circle in the hut's roof, but somehow he knew exactly what it was when it landed softly on top of his head.

"Don't move," whispered Dikemba.

And then another came, and another, and then a stream of butterflies poured down from the trees from all directions, hundreds of them falling like huge flakes of cobalt snow. Each of them fluttered toward Katook. They lightly set down on his face, his shoulders, his body, covering him, head to toe, in a slowly beating mass of papery wings. That is when Katook saw his family.

He saw himself back in Kattakuk, lying on a bed of thick grass, the sun on his face. Above him was a huge fig tree, heavy with swollen fruit. And way up in the tree, shaded by the wide, golden-veined fig leaves, were Kai and Lina. They were laughing and gorging themselves on the sweet figs. Katook rolled his head to one side and felt the soft, warm grass on his cheek. Drowsy, he looked over toward the trunk of the massive tree and saw his mother drifting off to sleep in his father's arms.

Then the dream suddenly ended, and Katook felt the butterflies lifting off one by one. He imagined them swirling overhead. With his eyes still closed, he saw them form a line that slowly vanished through the hole in the roof.

"Open your eyes," Dikemba whispered.

In a daze, Katook looked around, but there wasn't a butterfly in sight. And if it wasn't for the droplet of honey that slid into his mouth, he might have thought that the whole thing was just a dream.

"The voice at the heart of the world?" Katook said quietly, as much to himself as to the Boskii shaman.

Dikemba smiled.

"I saw blue butterflies. Then I dreamed of my home."

"Yes," replied Dikemba.

"I dreamed of something that happened a long time ago."

"Did you?" asked Dikemba with a long, slow blink of his almond-shaped eyes.

"Well, yes. I . . . I think so."

"Sometimes the voice is clear, the meaning less so," said Dikemba mysteriously. "But feel fortunate. The Creator has given you a dream." Then he began to sing, and the other Boskiis joined him until their voices filled the hut.

While the Boskiis sang in the nest, Katook began to climb down the tree. He could see Quigga and Sia grazing on ferns along the river.

Katook grabbed hold of a vine that fell toward the river and slid down face-first, until he was suspended just above the water's surface. Hanging by his tail, he lapped at the sweet, cold water, and as he drank, he felt his mind clear and the dream recede.

Suddenly a vivid blue reflection flashed before him. He looked up. A great sapphire-winged butterfly. It settled on a patch of velvety moss at the water's edge and satisfied its own thirst, its wings brilliant in the filtered sunlight. Iridescent blue when open, soft brown when closed.

Another butterfly flitted past Katook and joined the first. He chased after them, following them into the shade-dappled clearing where Quigga and Sia grazed.

Several more butterflies joined the pair, and then more, until hundreds circled overhead in an electric swirl of sapphire blue.

"That's right, Blue-Eyed One, watch, trust the call," he heard Dikemba say.

Katook saw that Dikemba and the other Boskiis were now lounging on the limbs of the banyan tree. Then, one by one, the butterflies began to depart in a long, lazy train that threaded itself eastward through the forest.

Katook turned back to Dikemba for a moment and wondered if what the shaman said was true—that he, Katook, could trust that he somehow *knew*. That maybe, just maybe, he wasn't cursed after all. That his eyes, blue as the sky, marked him not for his wrongdoing, but for something else. But for what?

"In time," Dikemba said, as if hearing Katook's question, "you will find your answers."

"Are you all right?" asked Quigga, who had walked up to Katook, with tiny Sia at his side.

"Yes, I'm fine."

"Then enough of this foolishness. Wave good-bye to your furry friends, and let's get out of this jungle. This way."

Quigga took a couple of steps, then stopped as he realized that Katook wasn't following him. "Oh, so that's it. You're going to stay with them," he said sarcastically. "Why not? Abandon your journey. Just give up."

Katook turned and looked up into the kind faces of the Boskiis. It was true, a part of him longed to stay with them, but he heard a cry in his heart that would not allow it.

"We should leave before darkness falls," Quigga insisted. "Follow me."

"No," Katook answered in a voice that surprised him as much as Quigga. "Follow me. It's this way." He pointed in the opposite direction from the one Quigga was taking.

"That's right, Blue-Eyed One, trust the call," he heard Dikemba say.

Quigga watched Katook bound away from him, leaping from branch to branch, heading off in the direction of the sapphire butterflies.

Sia gazed up at Quigga and said simply, "Go. And may the Creator keep you."

Quigga looked down at his small, tusked friend. "Come with us." Sia smiled and answered, "How could I do that and empty this jungle of all of its beauty?"

Quigga gently nuzzled her, then hurried after Katook, grumbling as he went. "I was born from a line of the finest quagga scouts ever to roam the plains. I have a better sense of direction than you will ever have in all of your confused, tree-climbing life! The only reason I'm following you is that for some ridiculous reason I care about you, and the idea of you wandering lost in this jungle all alone is simply too much for me to bear."

But of course, that was not the reason at all. Katook knew which way he was going, although not where, and though he might never admit it, Quigga knew that Katook knew.

They traveled deep into the rain forest, and the farther they went, the darker, swampier, and thicker the jungle became. Quigga was miserable. He slogged through gushy dark mud and picked his way through root- and log-strewn waterways, complaining the entire time. Meanwhile, Katook leapt joyously from branch to branch, his eyes fixed on the sapphire butterflies who flitted ahead of him.

Night and day, Katook felt eyes watching them from the wet black shadows. He heard the hungry growl of tigers, leopards, and panthers, and one evening he heard the heavy, winding slither of a python keeping pace with them. But never once did Katook feel afraid. He caught glimpses of the Great Ones, whom he knew were protecting them just as the Boskiis had promised they would.

"Great Ones, ha!" scoffed Quigga. "I don't see a thing."

"But—"

"And if I did, what kind of 'Great One' would chose to live in a place as far from great as this?"

And so they traveled like that for days, Katook in the lead, feeling safe and certain of their route, and Quigga, steeped in fear and discomfort, "looking out for them."

Chapter Fourteen
OG ASHAD

As the moist jungle air became lighter, Quigga's mood grew lighter with it. By the third day he was able to move with longer, quicker strides.

"At last," he said with a grand swish of his tail, "I can take a step or two without walking into a tree. Here, climb on my back," he told Katook. "We'll be out of these trees quicker if you ride. You have no idea of how badly I want to be out of this jungle."

So Katook hopped on Quigga's back and let him guide their way. But he was careful to make sure they kept following the sapphire-blue butterflies.

On the fourth day rays of sunlight speared through the trees, which, by now, were growing farther apart. And on the fifth day the forest opened onto a marshland and then a meadow that spread out in a vast pale green blanket sprinkled with tiny white flowers as far as Katook could see. At night it got so cold that the pair slept close together to keep warm, Quigga with his legs tucked under him, and Katook curled at his side.

As they traveled on, the flowers vanished and the grass lost its spongy feel and became hard and brown. They were climbing steadily now. The air grew thin and Katook found it harder to breathe. Their pace slowed, and Quigga complained endlessly. Even through these hardships—and even though Katook missed the trees and the familiarity of the Boskiis—the butterflies flew ahead of them, and Katook trusted that he was being guided in the right direction.

But guided toward what? he wondered. *And why me? And why Quigga, for that matter?*

Katook couldn't help but wonder if the course the butterflies were setting was his, and his alone. *But for what purpose? And if I'm being led, then who is leading me? The butterflies have shown me the way, but is it possible that something else is guiding them?*

The farther they traveled, the more Katook dreamed about his first encounter with Nadab. How he'd show Nadab the seal and, after one glance at it, she'd tell him that she knew exactly where there were others like him. "I'll take you there," she'd say. Then she would quickly pack her bags and lead Katook to his new home, where he would see lemurs everywhere and figs ripe on the trees. And where he would be so welcome.

One morning Katook woke up to find a dusting of fine, cold powder on his fur. When he touched it with his fingertip, it vanished. Flakes of the strange stuff were falling out of a white-gray sky.

"Snow," explained Quigga. "It's called snow. I've heard that it can be as deep as a river, as wide as a plain.

And I've also heard that many a
quagga has walked upon it and never returned.
That the sight of it alone can mean death for an
entire herd."

Katook stuck out his tongue and caught a piece
of it as it fell. He licked some from his fur. It had no taste.
"It seems harmless enough," he said.

"Never judge the many by the few," Quigga warned him.
"Isn't a single mosquito harmless? But put it in a swarm and
it can drop a lion. No, Katook, don't be deceived. There, look,
that's it, too."

Quigga jutted his nose toward mountain peaks rising jaggedly
in the distance. Katook saw that they were iced with white, as if
draped with clouds. Then he noticed something else,
and his heart lurched and his thoughts ran
in panicky circles.

"Quigga, the butterflies are gone."

"It's probably too cold for them.
It's too cold for me."

"But what are we going to do now?"

Quigga raised his withers in a brief shrug.
"We're going eastward. We might as well
keep going in that direction. We know
what's behind us. And I, for one, have
no desire to see either the rain forest
or the phorcus again."

"Maybe I can use what the Patah taught me
about the stars to guide us," Katook said. "Though the
sky is awfully cloudy . . ."

"There's nothing to worry about," Quigga told him. "Am I
not Quigga, son of Quilla,
son Quiloz, son of—"

"You are," Katook said quickly, not wanting to hear another recita-
tion of Quigga's lineage. "We'll go east."

The land became steeper and rockier. There were no trees,
no plants of any kind. Katook and Quigga ate snow for breakfast and

snow for dinner. They woke up and went to sleep hungry.
And the air was so thin that Katook felt dizzy and Quigga puffed
even at a walk.

Suddenly Katook's fur stood on end and Quigga came to a halt.

Just ahead, up on a rocky ledge, a snow leopard crouched, its eyes
locked on them. Its silver-white fur, marked with smoky blue-black
spots, shivered slightly as the leopard's taut muscles prepared to spring.

"Hang on," Quigga whispered.

Katook barely had time to grab hold of Quigga's mane when,
in a blur of white fur, the snow leopard attacked.

Quigga reared back, dug his hooves into the snowy ground, and
pushed off. In a heartbeat he was plunging through a shoulder-high
snowdrift and scrambling up a rocky path. Katook looked over
his shoulder and saw the leopard chasing after them, easily crossing
the snow on its broad white paws.

Quigga galloped across the snowy, rock-strewn
landscape. He leapt a narrow crevasse. Sprinted
up a field of gravel. Raced through a shallow
stream chunked with ice. But the snow
leopard kept after them. No matter which
course Quigga took, or how fast he ran,
the leopard kept pace with him, as if waiting
for him to grow weary so as to make the killing easier.
It seemed to Katook that it wasn't a matter of *if* the
leopard would leap onto Quigga's back and sink its teeth
into the quagga's neck, but *when*.

"We should split up," Quigga gasped through labored
breaths. "You can find shelter in the rocks."

"We've come this far. I'm not leaving you."

The leopard must have
sensed Quigga's weakness
because it quickened its pace.

Katook looked around, expecting to see
white fur and fangs leaping at him. But the
leopard had stopped running. It was crouched
low, snarling and hissing, but frozen in its tracks.

127

Amazed at their good fortune, Katook whispered, "I don't understand, but it's given up. It just stopped!"

"It's terrified. Look," Quigga said, his voice low and hoarse with awe.

Katook turned and instantly understood the snow leopard's fear. There in front of them was a caravan of tens of tusked, white woolly mammoths and sharp-horned black rhinoceroses. And sitting majestically on top of them, their golden fur shimmering in the sun—"Golden Monkeys," Katook said softly.

"They're not really golden. Actually, they're more of a sandy yellow," Quigga said under his breath.

They were close enough to smell the pungent wet odor of the woolly mammoths. Katook marveled at the elaborate polished armor and helmets that the monkeys wore, and the intricately gilded swords at their sides.

"Halt!" shouted the monkey who rode the lead mammoth.

"Oh, Quigga, it's them!" said Katook, thrilled. He called up to them, "Are you the Golden Monkeys of Og Ashad?"

"And if we are, what business is it of yours?" replied the leader of the regiment. His paw moved to his sheathed sword and rested there.

"All dressed up but crude manners," muttered Quigga.

"Shhh . . . ," whispered Katook as the leader scowled down at them.

"I am Morag, commander of the tenth legion of the Empress Og Bashana," he said in a haughty tone. "Who are you?"

"I'm Katook, and this is my friend Quigga. We're on

our way to Og Ashad," he continued a little nervously. "We're looking for a great explorer named Nadab. Perhaps you know her?"

But before the lead Golden Monkey could respond, another monkey hurried toward him, leaping from one white hide to the next. As he got closer Katook saw that he had an ice-white macaw with periwinkle feathers on his shoulder. The parrot stared intently at Katook while the monkey stopped directly behind Morag and spoke into his ear. Then Morag whispered something to the monkey, and the monkey, in turn, whispered something to the parrot, who lifted off and flew away.

Morag removed his hand from his sword and waved Katook and Quigga forward. "Indeed, I do know Nadab. A great explorer from Kolloboo, she is. Worthy of seeking out. We're on our way to Og Ashad now. Would you two like to join us?"

"Oh, yes," Katook said quickly, before Quigga could disagree.

"Then it will be my honor to escort you. Climb on, Little One, and make yourself comfortable! We'll reach Og Ashad before the sun sleeps."

Katook excitedly climbed up the woolly mammoth and into the pavilion that swayed atop its back. He stood on his hind legs, with his front paws resting on the open sill. He was beside himself with joy. *We did it!* he thought. *We followed the butterflies and now look at us—we're on our way to Nadab!*

From his high perch, Katook saw Quigga join the caravan, prancing and vainly tossing his mane from time to time in order to distinguish himself from the other pack animals. "We did it!" Katook yelled back to Quigga.

Hours passed as the caravan traveled on. Eventually Katook snuggled into the warmth of thick woolen blankets and, lulled by the swaying gait of the mammoth, he slipped into a dreamless sleep.

"Wake up. We're here." Katook had jerked awake to the sound of Morag's sharp voice. He scrambled up to see the commander pointing straight ahead of them.

The walled city seemed to rise straight up out of the mountain peak. Even from a distance, Katook marveled at its sharply sloping rooflines and soaring towers.

131

Thrilled at the sight of it, Katook leapt off the mammoth and ran back to Quigga. "Quigga, isn't it magnificent?" he asked breathlessly.

But Quigga just furrowed his brow as he looked up at the Golden Monkeys' city.

"What's wrong with you?" asked Katook. "We made it! Soon we'll meet Nadab. Soon we will each know our way."

Quigga had his eyes fixed on Og Ashad as he said simply, "It's too big."

Katook sighed. "You didn't like Kolloboo, you didn't like the rain forest. I suppose I shouldn't be surprised—"

"It's arrogant, is what it is," Quigga said softly. "It's as if the creatures who built it think themselves better than the world they live in.

As if they think that by building something like that on top of the mountain, they are more important than the mountain."

"But, Quigga, look at it . . . It's amazing!"

"Amazing, yes, but it is not beautiful."

The caravan climbed the wide cobblestone road that led up to city. Both sides of the road were lined with carved statues of Golden Monkeys in various poses of grandeur. One statue depicted a monkey, sword in hand, staring up at the sky. Another showed a monkey lounging on a bed of gold. And another was of a monkey with his arms spread wide, as if he were the reason the sun rose and set.

"Who do these monkeys think they are?" Quigga grumbled.

Katook ignored this grouchy comment and gazed up at the huge gates. Gates so tall and wide that the mammoths could enter two abreast. Perched on top of the gates, like enormous birds, were gilded stone warriors, their swords raised in triumph. And overshadowing all were the faces of huge Golden Monkeys that were carved into the city's stone towers.

Oddly, off to the side of the gates, as if cast off and forgotten, was an ancient wooden statue. It appeared far older than the rest, so old that the wood was petrified.

"Quigga, look, it's the Fossah!"

Quigga glanced briefly at the sculpture, but either he didn't recognize the Fossah's image or he was unmoved by it, because he simply shrugged and kept walking.

Morag noticed Katook's reverent expression. "One of our old gods. I can't remember his name."

"Fossah," replied Katook softly.

133

"That's right, Foss-ahh! I learned that as a pup,"
Morag proclaimed proudly. "The Foss-ahh, my
grandmother told me, was the first of all. But that was
long ago, and we've come far since then. There, look
at those." Morag proudly gestured at some of the
grander statues. "If I remember correctly, the one
to the left is Malattay, then comes Silooch, Timol,
Idda, and Yisov—ancient gods from back in the days
before we worshiped our ancestors."

"You worship yourselves?" Katook asked incredulously.

"We worship power, and since none are more powerful
than ourselves, it's only natural. Wouldn't you agree?"

"Humble folk, aren't they?" Quigga muttered under
his breath.

But Katook remained silent as Morag spoke a password
to the guards, the great gates swung open, and they entered
the walled city.

The streets were so carefully paved in stone, each block
perfectly cut and set next to the one beside it, that they
seemed to be made of one seamless block of polished rock.

The buildings were tall as mountains, with high arches
and gabled roofs. Intricate stonework of gargoyles
and ornamental carvings covered every surface. Gold and
gemstones glittered from doorways and windowsills.
And everywhere the gigantic carved monkeys gazed down
on all who passed below.

"Oh, Quigga," Katook murmured, "have you ever seen
such a place?"

"No, and I hope I never do again. These stones are
murder to walk on, and I think I have a pebble stuck
in my right front hoof. I don't care what you say, I don't
trust this place. I can't wait to find this Nadab fellow—"

"Nadab isn't a fellow," Katook pointed out.
"She's a female."

"I don't care if Nadab is a cockroach. I just want
to see *her* and get out of here."

Just then Katook saw a group of elegantly

135

dressed Golden Monkeys and palace guards approaching from the end of the long street. They all looked much alike, their expressions serene and their fur shimmering, brushed to an impossible luster. They seemed wonderfully elegant with their calm expressions and easy grace.

"Oh, but look how beautiful they all are. Their fur truly is made of gold."

"Beautiful?" Quigga scoffed. "Don't make me laugh. They're hideous."

"You're just jealous, afraid that they're as stunning as you are!"

"Jealous? Ha! They are chubby, unfriendly fur-toes!"

Katook ended their argument by greeting the Golden Monkeys who were almost upon them. "Hello! What a beautiful place this is!"

But not only didn't they respond, they didn't even bother to meet his gaze as they walked past him.

"I'm telling you," Quigga whispered. "Something isn't right here."

"Oh, stop it, Quigga," said Katook, trying to squash his own seeds of doubt. "I'm sure it's nothing. They just didn't hear me. You're imagining things."

"You don't need to see a panther to sense that it's there." Quigga's nostrils flared. "Speaking of which—"

Their discussion was interrupted by Morag, who had climbed down from his perch. Now he stood gesturing toward the largest and most magnificent of the buildings. It towered over a vast courtyard with an enormous fountain. Saber-toothed tigers guarded the stairs to the building, their huge curved teeth shining brilliant white.

"The Empress's Palace!" Morag proclaimed. He clapped his fat paws, and suddenly the tigers bounded from their posts and formed two lines.

Katook gazed at the path between them, which ended in front of the palace doors. "For me?" he asked, taken aback by the grand gesture.

"Of course," answered Morag. "You're here to see the Empress, aren't you?"

"Actually I'm here to see—"

"—of course, Nadab," interrupted Morag. "But wouldn't you first like to meet the Empress?"

Thrilled, Katook answered, "Well, yes, but—"

"Then let's not keep her waiting," said Morag. He took Katook's arm and started leading him toward the palace doors.

Feeling very important and excited, Katook spoke over his shoulder to Quigga. "See, I told you everything would be fine."

But Quigga didn't answer.

Katook turned around. Quigga wasn't there. Back by the caravan, a Golden Monkey looped a braided rope around his neck and started to lead him away.

"Where are you taking Quigga?" asked Katook.

"To be looked after," Morag assured him. "Look how he favors his left hoof. Wouldn't you rather your friend be given food and drink and have his hoof attended to before he meets the Empress?"

"Yes, of course, but—"

"Then don't worry. Your friend will be fine. Now come along. The Empress awaits you . . . "

But Quigga was not fine. With the rope tight around his neck and another around his forelegs, two Golden Monkey guards dragged him, kicking and screaming, down a long, dark tunnel that ended someplace far below the walled city.

Choking from the noose around his throat, Quigga struggled to speak. "Where are you taking me?"

The Golden Monkeys didn't answer.

"Release me!" Quigga managed to say. "I am a quagga!"

"Oh, my," said one of the monkeys, "a quagga!" Then the two monkeys broke out in laughter.

The tunnel took a sharp turn, and they came to a huge, dimly lit corral. Inside it zebras and deer, blackbuck and pronghorn antelopes, bearded pigs and pygmy hippos, wild horses and chickens and a pair of okapi with their baby were all crowded together.

"What is this?" Quigga yelled as one of the guards locked the corral gates behind him. "What kind of place is this? Let me out of here!"

"You're in the castle of Og Ashad. Well, beneath it, anyway," the guard replied with a laugh, and strode away.

Quigga turned to face the others in the crowded corral. "What's wrong with you?" he demanded. "Why don't you fight?"

"Where would we go?" asked a sad-eyed, spiral-horned blackbuck.

Another spoke in a voice so low and broken Quigga could barely hear him. "This place is not a castle, it's a prison. And the only ones free to wander in this gilded cage are the Golden Monkeys. The rest of us are their beasts of burden."

"I'll be no slave to anyone," said Quigga defiantly.

"You will in time. Look at us. Do any of us look free to you?" asked a pronghorn.

"But we came so far . . . Do any of you know Nadab, the scientist?"

"Scientist? Ha!" said the blackbuck. "Nadab is no more than a warden. Always poking us, weighing us, measuring us. I relieve myself on the ground she walks on."

Quigga's shoulders sank. "What will become of me?"

"You will work for them," someone answered.

"You are one of theirs now," replied another.

Chapter Fifteen
IN THE PALACE

Taking Katook by his wrist, Morag gently led him through the palace. The corridor they crossed was cavernous and spare, with high, vaulted ceilings. Orange-lime sunlight flooded through tinted windows that were as tall as fig trees. At the far end of this grand hall was an arched passageway that opened into a jeweled, domed chamber.

Katook bit back a gasp. In the chamber's very center, Empress Og Bashana and her daughter, the Princess Jallia, sat on thrones carved from ebony that rested upon single blocks of snow-white stone. And on either side of them were two magnificent hyacinth macaws, tethered to their perches. One stretched out its wing. The tip had been clipped off, all flight gone forever. The Empress and her daughter were flanked by more guards, some holding black leopards on chained leashes. The leopards let out a low growl.

Morag gave Katook's wrist a firm tug and whispered, "Come." As they slowly crossed the throne room, Katook felt the leopards' cruel eyes fixed on him.

The Empress looked briefly at the familiar ice parrot, which now perched on the Princess's arm, then cut an appraising glance at Katook. "What have we here? Is this the 'treasure' you brought me?"

Morag bowed low and answered, "The mammoths and rhinoceroses are being unloaded in the viewing hall as we speak. But I thought you might be interested in this," he said with a gesture toward Katook. "Step forward."

"Me?" asked Katook.

"Do as you're told," insisted Morag in a harsh whisper. "Forward!"

Katook squared his shoulders and bravely obeyed. The Empress squinted at him; then a wave of anger washed over her chubby face.

"What is this, Morag?" she said with displeasure. "Don't I already have one of these?" She pointed at a guard who stood in the shadows of a vestibule. "You, fetch me Nadab."

At last! thought Katook with excitement. *At last I'll finally meet the famous explorer!*

The Empress turned back to Morag, her eyes bright with fury.

"Please don't tell me that you have been gone these past ten moon-treads, at my expense, to return with something I already possess!" She stood and stabbed her finger in Katook's direction. "Tell me, Morag, that this rodent is not your finest prize from the east!"

"But Your H-highness," Morag stammered as he pressed his forehead into the stone floor. "His eyes. I thought his eyes would please you."

"His eyes?"

"Yes, Your Majesty. They are blue."

"Closer," she commanded Katook.

As he took his first step he heard chains rattling and knew that the leopards had crouched, ready to leap at the Empress's command.

Princess Jallia stepped down from her throne. She turned to the leopards and whispered, "Shhh . . . " She circled Katook as if she were inspecting a prize statue. Then she lifted his chin with her chubby little forefinger.

"Oh, Mama, look! They are the most beautiful blue."

Katook felt a little embarrassed by all this attention. *Dikemba was right,* he thought. *My eyes aren't a curse after all. She said they were beautiful.*

Just then a robed Kolloboo entered, her face buried in a large, leather-bound book.

"Nadab," said the Empress. "Do we have a blue-eyed one of these in the collection?"

"Your Highness?" the scientist responded, sounding distracted.

"This thing standing before me," said the Empress impatiently. "Do we own one with blue eyes?"

Nadab approached Katook and glanced at him without interest.

"Nadab," he whispered excitedly. "I've come to see you."

But Nadab's only response was to poke Katook in the ribs and roughly turn his head from side to side as she looked into his ears. She turned to the Empress. "No, Your Highness, we don't have one of these. The blue eyes may be unusual for its kind—I will catalog them, of course—but in my opinion they do not make this specimen particularly valuable."

"Thank you, you may go."

"But my seal . . . ," Katook said to Nadab as she turned away. "My seal! Please, I've traveled so far to see you!"

In one motion Nadab suddenly snapped the string around Katook's neck and ripped off his pouch and seal. Katook felt his heart quicken with hope as she pulled an ink case from a bag at her hip, dabbed the cylinder on the inky sponge, and rolled it across a blank page in her journal.

Katook looked on expectantly as Nadab read the message.

"You see," Katook began to explain. "I came from—"

He stopped as Nadab casually tossed the ceramic seal on the floor, closed her journal, and began walking away.

"Wait!" said the Empress. "What was the message?"

"It is a message from the Kolloboo. They have sent him and the quagga who accompanied him to you as gifts. With their compliments."

"G-gifts?" Katook stammered. "But I—"

"I know," Nadab interrupted him. "It said, 'He seeks those like himself. Can you show him the way?'"

"Then, Nadab, do as you have been bid," the Empress said with a cruel smile. "Show him the way to those like himself."

"Yes, Your Highness," said Nadab with a bow.

She motioned to a guard, who gripped Katook by the scruff of his neck and led them to a small anteroom. They started down a steep, dimly lit stairway.

Katook felt confused and dumb. He repeated the Kolloboo's message to himself, over and over again. He couldn't understand Nadab's rudeness and disinterest in him or the guard's roughness.

"Is it true?" asked Katook hesitantly. "Are you really bringing me to those like myself?"

Nadab looked into Katook's expectant eyes then answered coldly, "Like yourself? You say that as if you know what it means—like yourself—as though you have any idea who you are. The arrogance of your stupidity appalls me."

"But all I want is a place with other lemurs where I can feel at home again."

"Home? Don't make me laugh. Home is not a place. It's not some cozy little room with soft-eyed stupid creatures who look like you. Lee-murs . . . so that's what you're called. Well, listen hard, my blue-eyed friend, home is knowledge."

"You're wrong. It's more than that. Home is a place . . . a feeling. It's—"

Nadab shut him up with a harsh, "No. Home is knowledge, nothing more."

Broken, Katook shuffled down the stone steps after the Kolloboo explorer. *I've come all this way for nothing! She's not going to help me. I'll never find another lemur as long as I live.*

Down and down they went, into the dark bowels of the city. The only sounds were their footsteps on the rough stone and the candles spitting wax against the blackened walls of the stairwell.

Katook wanted to speak but didn't know what to say. His eyes welled with tears and he lost track of how far they descended into the mountain. Finally he asked, "Where's my friend?"

"Yes, the quagga," Nadab said in a clipped tone. "Kin to the zebras, solid-hoofed, partly striped, swift runner, plains dweller, approximately forty-eight paw-widths to the shoulder . . ."

"His name is Quigga. We arrived together. He has brown stripes—"

"Never mind," said Nadab as she turned a corner. "I'm sure he's down here someplace."

"Where are you taking me?" asked Katook, suddenly feeling more afraid with each step.

"We're almost there" was all Nadab said in return.

Katook smelled their destination before they reached it. The odor was rank with unwashed animals. If there was a smell of despair, this was it, he thought. At last they came to a wide tunnel, crudely carved into the bedrock of the mountain. It was lined on both sides with cages and corrals.

Katook had never seen such a collection of creatures. There were owl-faced monkeys and sinkabous and mangabeys and white-handed gibbons. They all seemed to be grouped in the cages according to how closely they resembled each other.

"Here," said Nadab as a guard unlocked a cage. "Here is your home."

Katook quickly glanced inside. It was filled with coatimundi, raccoons, red pandas, and other animals, but not a single lemur. "They all have rings on their tails, but—" Katook began.

"—but there are no lemurs here," Nadab finished for him. "That's true. The last one died. But look around. The animals here are enough like you."

Katook tried to run, but the Golden Monkey guard grabbed him and threw him to the ground. Nadab stood over him. "Where do you think you'd run to?"

He was shaking so hard that he wasn't sure he could speak.

"Consider yourself special," Nadab went on. "You're the only lemur in all of Og Ashad." Then she turned to the Golden Monkey.

"Into the cage with him."

The guard heaved him. Katook landed on a pile of wet straw. As he rolled over and wiped the soggy, smelly mess from his face, he heard the cage door clang shut.

"Let me out of here!" he shouted.

But Nadab and the guard walked away.

"Let me out!"

"Be careful what you ask for," said Nadab over her shoulder. The guard laughed.

141

Chapter Sixteen
ANOTHER CHANCE

Katook started madly climbing the bars of the cage. Back and forth, up and down, faster and faster. Screaming. There was no way out. But that didn't stop him. He bounded off the walls, climbed up ramps and over sleeping boxes, lost in the nightmare of his imprisonment.

Gamic was right, Katook screamed inside his head. *I'm nothing but a cursed outcast. What was I thinking, following butterflies! What a fool!*

Exhausted, Katook curled up into a tight ball on the foul-smelling floor.

A very shy voice whispered, "Excuse me."

Katook rolled over and saw a creature about half his size squatting at the base of the cage door. It was a very young ring-tailed cat with fawn-gray fur, large gentle eyes, and a dainty pointed muzzle.

"Bidis is my name," said the little creature timidly. "I don't want to be rude, especially since you seem upset enough as it is. But that particular filthy spot you're curled up on in this exceptionally filthy cage is mine."

Katook wiped bits of dry grass from his face and stared at the shy, fastidious being who called himself Bidis. "Is it?" said Katook, both bewildered and amused.

"Clearly there are many other filthy spots just like it," the little being said encouragingly. "And if you'd like, I'd be happy to help you find one. But that one, the one you are presently occupying, is mine."

"How about this spot?" kidded Katook, pointing to a spot on the floor less than an arm's-length away.

"All yours," answered Bidis seriously. "And just so you know, I don't snore, kick in my sleep, or belch very much. And you?"

"No," answered Katook. "At least I've never been told that I do."

142

"Of course," Bidis said with a slow, grave nod of his neat little head.

Katook glanced around the cramped, dimly lit room. Most of the animals were sleeping; some were listlessly cleaning themselves, and others gazed straight ahead with blank stares. The air was thick and humid. There were no windows.

"How long have you been in this place?" asked Katook.

"I don't know really. Time is hard to tell down here. We never see the golden ball, or the silver orb."

Stunned, Katook began, "You never . . . you don't go outside ever?"

"Oh, no," answered Bidis. "Some of the larger, stronger animals work outside, but the rest of us stay here always."

"I don't understand . . . Why?"

"Because that is how they like it" was the answer Bidis gave. "If you'll excuse me, it's time for me to sleep." And the little creature pulled himself into a tight ball and closed his large eyes.

Feeling lost and broken, Katook closed his eyes as well and listened carefully for the voice inside him that had spoken so clearly when he was with the Boskiis. But all he could hear were the sounds of snoring and wheezing. He felt farther than ever from finding the home he sought. And worst of all, he'd led Quigga into this prison.

Doing his best not to wake those around him, especially Bidis, Katook tossed and turned. He rolled and tumbled. He tried every position he had ever slept in and many he'd never tried before, but he couldn't sleep. And when he finally did fall asleep, he didn't snore or belch, but he kicked, as if he might kick his way through the bars of the cage to freedom.

Sometime later, Katook woke feeling the scorch of fire. He opened his eyes to find himself staring into flames only inches from his face. He heard, "I've got him!" As the torch was pulled away he realized he was being held by a Golden Monkey guard. Behind the guard stood another Golden Monkey, this one female and elegantly attired.

144

"Take it outside," said the elegant one. "And be careful not to harm it."

"At once," answered the guard as he marched Katook through the pen of sleeping animals, kicking them out of his way.

"Where are you taking me?" asked Katook, still groggy from sleep.

"Silence!" yelled the bejeweled Golden Monkey, whose name, Katook later discovered, was Glippia. "Do not speak unless you are spoken to. If you understand me, nod your head."

Frightened, Katook nodded.

He was led back up the long, winding stairway then down a hall lined with tapestries of Golden Monkeys in grand poses. They stopped at a door inlaid with diamonds and gold.

Glippia gently tapped on the heavy door and it swung open, revealing a large room made entirely of rose-colored quartz. The floor, walls, even the ceiling shimmered in a pale polished pink. The room was lit by hundreds of candles, some of them as tall as Katook. In the center of the chamber was a bathtub carved out of a single block of night-black onyx, filled with steaming, jasmine-scented water.

Glippia motioned to the guard, who quickly slipped away; then she clapped her hands. Six tiny marmoset monkeys entered, balancing three large golden trays holding colored ribbons, bottles of scents, brushes, and plush towels. They set the trays by the tub, then stood back, their paws clasped obediently in front of them.

"Get in the tub," Glippia told Katook.

"But—" started Katook, feeling dread. *Water. Again!*

"Rodent!" screamed the Golden Monkey. "Don't make me say it twice!"

Katook climbed into the steaming bath. The instant he slipped into the water, he felt the marmosets' tiny paws all over him, washing, scrubbing, and brushing every part of his body.

"Now get out," ordered Glippia.

Katook did so. And before he could say a word, the marmosets quickly wrapped him in plush towels. They dried, fluffed, and brushed his fur until it gleamed. Then they tied ribbons in his fur and sprayed him with so much scent he felt dizzy.

"Turn it around," Glippia commanded the tiny monkeys.

They led Katook to the front of a large polished stone with a

mirrorlike surface. He was stunned silent. He hardly recognized himself. Finally he said, as much to himself as the others, "I look ridiculous."

Silently, Glippia paced back and forth behind Katook, scrutinizing the marmosets' work. She adjusted a single ribbon and pronounced, "It will do."

She started toward a doorway and without even a backward glance, said, "Come." Knowing he had no choice, he obeyed.

They passed through a hallway and entered a fragrant room that was hung with sheer panels of pink fabric. They reminded Katook of flower petals, and standing there, surrounded by them, he felt as if he were standing inside a giant pink blossom.

"Come to me," said a voice from somewhere inside the flower. "Let me get a good look at my new blue-eyed pet."

Katook pushed through the pink fabric and found Princess Jallia lounging on a pink divan, her head resting on a pile of pink pillows.

She smiled at the sight of him. "How sweet!" she said, clapping her paws. "How stunningly special! Do you have a name, you adorable little blue-eyed pet of mine?"

"Katook," he answered quietly. He didn't like the idea of being anyone's pet but sensed it would be unwise to object.

"And what a cute little name it is!" said the Princess cheerfully. "Tell me about you, Katoofie. Entertain me with a story. How did you come to be here?"

"Princess," Katook began, wincing at the nickname, "I will tell you everything, and I will make the telling of it as entertaining as I can. But first, please, my friend was taken away. Where is he?"

"Your friend?" said the Princess disinterestedly.

"He's a quagga. Very handsome. When we arrived—"

"Oh, him," interrupted the Princess, sounding bored. She sat up and stretched, and two tiny marmoset handmaids rushed to fluff her pillows.

"He was taken away," continued Katook. "Please help me find him."

"I'm sure your friend is fine. He must have been taken to the livestock pens," replied the Princess.

"May I see him?"

"Possibly, but not tonight."

"But—"

"Enough," she said, as only a Princess can. "And I refuse to have my playthings talking back to me. Am I clear?"

"Yes," answered Katook, frightened by the sudden flash of anger in her eyes.

"Good. Because it would hurt me greatly to be forced to discipline you." Katook saw her handmaids cringe at those words. "Now come, sit by my side and tell me a story."

Katook reluctantly sat on the floor beside the divan, and the Princess rewarded him with a ripe, fresh fig. Katook held the precious fruit in his paw, awed. It had been such a long time since he had held such a treat.

"You need not worship it," teased the Princess with a small laugh. "You may eat it."

But as Katook bit into the fig and tasted its sweetness, he was torn between delight and guilt. Thoughts of his family flooded into him. He couldn't help but wonder if they, along with all of Bo-hibba, were still suffering under the Long Winter.

"I traveled across a wide, blue sea on the back of a sea turtle," he began. "And when I finally woke from a deep sleep, I was farther from home than any in my village had ever been before . . ."

As Katook told the tale of his journey, the Princess's eyes gradually drifted shut. When he heard her snore, he crept silently to the window seat. Gripping the iron grillwork that covered the window, he gazed out. Except for a few flickering candles, the city was dark. And there, high in the Princess's turret, he curled up and stared out across the dark and lonely silence of Og Ashad and thought, *Quigga was right. This place is not beautiful at all.*

The days melted into each other as Katook told stories to the Princess. One morning he woke in the window seat. The sun was rising over the saw-toothed walls of the city, sending sharp bars of light down into the vacant streets. He heard a loud crack, followed by the sound of wheels rolling across cobblestones. Then a long, distorted shadow of what looked like a horse slowly splayed out across an empty plaza, and right after it came the most painful thing Katook had ever seen. It was Quigga pulling a dung wagon.

His once glossy hide was matted and filthy. His head hung low as a fierce Golden Monkey cracked a whip across his welted haunches.

"Quigga . . . . ," Katook called from the turret. But Quigga was too far away to hear him. "Quigga . . . ," Katook said again, but only to himself as he watched the Golden Monkey whip his proud, vain friend.

"Come here, my blue-eyed pet." Katook heard the Princess call to him as she stirred in her bed. "Come tell me another wonderful story. I like waking up and falling asleep to a magical tale. You'll tell me two a day. Keep them fresh and exciting."

Tears of despair clouded Katook's eyes as he watched Quigga slowly cross the plaza. "Where are you hiding, my precious Katoofie?" called the Princess. "Today we'll have your bows changed. Blue bows. Blue to match your eyes. Come to Jallia," she wheedled. "I have another sweet fig for you."

Katook stayed at the window, his heart breaking as Quigga disappeared down an alley and out of sight. Then, just as he was about to go to the Princess, something caught his eye. It was a single, sapphire butterfly. The butterfly flew right past the turret window and then vanished.

It's not real, thought Katook. *It's only my imagination.*

But the butterfly circled back and fluttered outside the iron grillwork that covered the window, hovering just in front of Katook.

"Go away!" Katook said angrily. "I'm a prisoner dressed up like one of my sister's playthings, and my best friend is beaten while I'm given figs to eat!"

"Who are you talking to?" asked the Princess.

Katook ignored her and continued ranting at the butterfly. "Look at where following you has brought me!"

The butterfly paused a moment, then flew into the room. It was circling over Katook's head when the Princess pushed through a panel of fabric.

"You should come when I call you," she scolded. Then she noticed the butterfly and her face brightened. "Catch it for me! Hurry, before it flies back out again!"

Katook looked up and saw the brilliant wings beating gently as the butterfly flew round and round, just above his head, like a moving sapphire halo. For a reason he couldn't explain, he began to feel a sense

149

"Your Highness . . . ?" said Glippia.

Then the butterfly flew toward the Princess. It danced in the air around the finger she pointed at Katook, and then, amazingly, instead of trying to pluck the butterfly from the air, Jallia held her finger steady. The butterfly lightly touched down on the very tip of it.

"Oh," the Princess breathed softly as the butterfly's sapphire wings slowly opened and closed.

After a moment the butterfly weightlessly took flight, flitted behind a pink panel, and vanished.

"Oh, how strange," Jallia whispered. "It came to me. Nothing has ever come to me by itself before. How beautiful—"

"Your Highness," Glippia said again. "You called for me?"

"L-leave us . . . ," the Princess stammered. She looked at Katook, and he felt an unexpected surge of hope.

Katook waited until Glippia and the guards were gone before he said, "Princess, my life is in your hands. So I'm asking you to please set me and my friend free."

"And why would I do such a thing?"

Katook hesitated, searching for persuasive words and finding only simple truth. "Because you have the power to do it," he said. "And you know it's the right thing to do."

The Princess studied Katook. "Captives do not tell the Princess what is right and wrong," she informed him, but as she spoke, he heard something soft and curious in her voice. And the look in her eyes seemed less angry. It was then that Katook realized that he had a chance. That maybe, just maybe, she might not throw him back into the cage to die a lonely death. That perhaps the sapphire butterfly had arrived for this very reason.

The Princess walked over to Katook and stared at him for a long moment. Then, without a word, she began slowly removing the ribbons from his fur. When the last of the ribbons was gone, she handed him a collar woven from golden mesh.

"What's this?" Katook eyed the collar with distrust.

"You must put it on. When you wear it in the city, everyone will assume you're on a royal errand. No one will stop you."

Katook felt his heart beating hard with hope. "And my friend?"

"Stay here until I call for you."

of comfort and hopefulness that he hadn't had since he'd been with the Boskiis and, before that, back in the cave on Bo-hibba.

"Reach up and grab it!" commanded the Princess.

Katook looked at her a moment, then said, "I can't."

"Of course you can. Just reach up and grab it."

"No, this," said Katook, and he waved his arm across the room. "I can't live like this. I'm not a pet. While my friend hauls dung and is beaten, I tell stories and am rewarded with figs. This is not what I want. It's not who I am."

The Princess stared at Katook, her eyes wide with shock. "You dare speak to me like this? Glippia!" she screamed.

Footsteps rushed down the hall toward them and Glippia, flanked by a pair of guards, hurried into the room.

"This—" the Princess began, pointing at Katook, "take it—" But she fell silent as the brilliant sapphire butterfly settled on Katook's paw, opening and closing its wings.

Katook waited all morning and into the afternoon before the Princess returned.

"Is he all right?" Katook asked anxiously.

She quickly closed the door behind her. Then she crossed the room and pushed aside a tapestry, revealing a hidden stairway. "Hurry."

"But Quigga—" he started as they hurried down the stairs.

"His wounds have been cleaned and he's been given fresh water and food."

"But are you sure he's all right?"

"I'm told he's tired. But he can walk."

They entered a dark, narrow hallway that seemed to go on for a very long time. At the end of it Katook saw a small arched door. The Princess paused, her hand on the knob. Then she held out the pouch Katook had worn around his neck. "You'll find your friend in the alley on the other side of this door," she said hurriedly. "I can't go out there. And I can't be seen with you."

"Thank you," he said, taking the pouch.

"No need for that. Now go quickly!"

They shared a brief smile. She was about to go, but turned back. "Katook, go with the gods." Then she hurried away.

Katook quietly opened the door and stepped out into the alley. A painfully thin quagga was bent over, slowly drinking fresh water from an earthen bowl.

"Quigga?" Katook whispered.

Quigga looked up, his eyes brimming with tears.

Katook rushed to his friend and hugged him tightly around the neck. "I was so frightened for you. Oh . . . this scar . . ." Katook's paw trembled as he traced a brand the Golden Monkeys had burned into Quigga's haunch.

"That large-nosed Boskii should get a good whiff of me now," Quigga said with a half smile.

Then he and Katook began winding their way through the alleys and streets of Og Ashad, heading toward the main gates and, beyond them, freedom.

If it hadn't been for the jewel that fell from Empress Og Bashana's necklace, Katook and Quigga would have escaped Og Ashad without incident. But for a reason that only the Fossah knows, a ruby dislodged itself from the Empress's necklace and bounced twice on the stone floor before landing on the Empress's cat. The cat violently shook it off, sending the jewel soaring—a sparkling fat oval of light, too tempting for the ice parrot, who sat perched on the window ledge. With a graceful swoosh of periwinkled white feathers and black beak, the bird plucked the jewel from the air and carried it once around the room, evading the Empress's angry reach, before sailing out the window.

And if the ice parrot hadn't lost its beaky grip on the ruby and let it drop toward the street far below, and if the Empress hadn't looked down from her window, she would never have noticed Katook and Quigga silently making their way toward the gates of Og Ashad.

"Guards!" the Empress called out. "Guards!"

She threw open her door, and as she stepped out she almost ran into Princess Jallia, who was sneaking back to her room. One glance at the guilty look on her daughter's face, and the Empress grabbed her by the wrist. "You did this!"

"But, Mother—"

"How dare you release my beasts!" railed the Empress.

Just then four of the Empress's Golden Monkey guards bounded up the stairs, each of them with a predator on a chain. "The lemur and the quagga are escaping as I speak," she said to her brutal minions. "Fetch them."

"Alive?" asked one of the guards.

"If possible. If not—"

"Mother!"

The Empress aimed her hard, regal gaze on her daughter. "Silence," she hissed. "You've done enough harm. Now go to your room!"

Princess Jallia bowed her head. As she walked away, she heard her mother's final orders to the guards. "Do what you will. Now go!"

They fled silently through the stone-quiet city. Katook was keenly aware that if they were spotted, they'd never escape the Empress's guards and their beasts. Especially now, because Quigga—tired, beaten, his flanks burning from the whip—could barely walk.

"Please, hurry," Katook whispered, urging him on. "I know how much you must hurt and how tired you are, but we have to keep going. It's not far now. Look!" He pointed toward the spires of Og Ashad's huge main gates.

"Leave me," Quigga said. "I'm slowing you down."

"Not another word about that. Now come on."

"All I want to do is stop and rest for a while."

"You can rest all you like once we're out of—" Katook began, but suddenly he heard the steady rhythm of large, padded paws moving down the narrow stone street.

Katook whirled and felt terror freeze his limbs. The Golden Monkeys' beasts—leopards, hyenas, wolves, and cheetahs—were racing toward them with blinding speed.

"Get on!" yelled Quigga.

It was only a matter of minutes before the Empress's snarling beasts would tear into Quigga's haunches and drag

them both to the ground. *We've come this far to die like this,* Katook thought helplessly.

As Quigga bolted, citizens and slaves scrambled to get out of their way. The quagga stumbled over a basket, and his knees buckled under him.

Katook lost his grip on Quigga's mane and slammed hard into a stone wall. Dizzy, the air knocked from his chest, he staggered to his feet. Though the ground felt as if it were tilting beneath him, Katook could see that the city gates were only a short distance away.

"We're almost there!" he yelled as he scrambled back up onto his friend's back. But Quigga was in a daze and stumbled slowly toward the gates. Even if they made it before they were torn to pieces, the gates were locked and guarded. There was no way out of the city.

Still, Katook couldn't give up. "Keep running!" he urged Quigga as they staggered forward.

And then a very curious thing happened.

The gates swung open to admit another train of woolly mammoths. Quigga summoned

what little strength he had and, in a burst of speed, squeezed past the mammoth caravan.

Katook heard Quigga's lungs wheezing and one of the Golden Monkeys shouting to the guards to keep the gates open. "Escapees!" he yelled.

"It's no good," Quigga panted. "I can't run anymore."

A thunderous crash echoed behind them. Katook spun around as a great section of the city's wall crumbled, enormous blocks of stone tumbling into the streets. Undaunted, a pack of the giant wolves leapt and clawed its way over the rubble. Another section of wall came crashing down, then another and another.

Katook looked back through the choking dust and saw the wolves trapped in a mountain of tumbled stone. They looked frightened, their tails between their legs, their heads low. The walls continued falling around them.

Obeying her mother's orders, Princess Jallia was on her way to her chamber when she heard the rumbling outside. She hurried to a window.

154

At first all she could see was a dense cloud of dust lit from behind by searing sunlight. It made her eyes sting. But then, as the dust started to clear, she could make out the blurry mounds of rubble as the city walls continued to fall, revealing huge stretches of the green fields beyond. Near the city gates, she saw the wolves huddled together, surrounded by fallen stone. In the streets, the inhabitants of Og Ashad screamed and ran. Frightened, confused, they were desperate to flee. Her mother's fearsome guards seemed as confused as everyone else.

We built our fortress for a thousand generations, and in only minutes it is coming apart, Princess Jallia thought. *How bold we are. How stupid.*

Her reflections turned to Katook and Quigga. Would her little blue-eyed pet somehow find his way to freedom? In the midst of the wailing destruction of her city, she was struck with a certainty she could never explain. *They will make it. They will escape. I'm sure of it.*

Princess Jallia headed for a stairway that led out of the palace. She took the stairs two by two, hoping to catch a last glimpse of them. Strangely, though she knew that she ought to be afraid of being crushed by falling rock, she wasn't frightened at all.

She started running, leaping over rubble and weaving through the crowds. She was almost to the gates when quite suddenly the city fell silent. Through a creamy haze of dust, Princess Jallia saw what looked like an enormous tail. It swished quickly around the ruins of Og Ashad's great gates and vanished from sight.

The Princess dropped to her knees and drew in a sharp breath. She felt as if some enormous presence were watching her, a being she had no words for. Then, directly in front of her, she saw immense paw prints deep in the stones of the courtyard. She tried to shake her disbelief. A creature with a tail and paws so huge that it dwarfed the wolves and the tigers and even the mammoths. A creature so powerful that it left tracks in stone.

155

Gently, she reached out and laid her small paws inside the prints. She closed her eyes, realizing that Katook had told the truth—letting them go was the right thing to do.

Katook never knew how they escaped; only that they did. He and Quigga made it across the grassy plateau outside the fortress city, through a copse of trees, and onto a wide plain of low grass that seemed to go on forever. In two days Og Ashad was far behind them, and though they kept moving, they had no idea where they were going, or why they were going there. Katook didn't care. Ever since his time with the Boskiis, he found that the where or the why of things didn't seem to matter as much as it once had. He thought: *It's enough that we're safe and free, and that I have a friend, and that the sun is warm on our backs.*

On the third night away from Og Ashad, finally feeling safe,

Katook and Quigga slowed their pace. The full moon seemed to Katook to be as fat and pleasurable as a good memory.

Katook snuffed at the air. "This feels like a good place to sleep," he said as he admired the view from the edge of the plateau. Below them, as far as he could see, was a vast plain, dotted with shimmering pools of moonlight.

"It's as wide as the big blue," he told Quigga. He paused. "Which way do you think we should go tomorrow?"

Quigga cut nervous glances at Katook, but mostly he stared out at the empty plain below them. Then he lay down and folded his legs beneath him. He had been so quiet, for so long, that Katook thought some part of his spirit was broken and would need time to heal.

"Katook?" Quigga said at last.

"Yes?"

"There's something I have to tell you."

Katook waited silently.

"I once told you that I was a great quagga scout, like my father, and his father, and on and on as far back as memory holds."

"Yes, I remember."

"Well, it's not true," said Quigga with difficulty. "What is true is that I come from a long line of quagga scouts, but unlike them, I have no sense of direction. I never have. And I lied to you when I said that I sprained my leg. The truth is that I paused too long at a watering hole and when I looked up, my herd was gone. I thought I would catch up to them, but I set out in the wrong direction. I was lost when I found you, but I was too ashamed to tell you."

Katook gently stroked Quigga's chest but remained silent.

"You must think horribly of me," said Quigga.

"No," said Katook. "You're my friend. And you're a quagga. You'll find your way."

"Do you think so?" asked Quigga.

"I do," answered Katook with a smile. "I know it."

Katook didn't stop stroking Quigga's chest until he felt his friend's breathing soften into sleep. Then Katook rolled onto his back and stared up at the stars. He remembered how fascinated the Kolloboo were by the mystery of the needle-guide, but how little they understood its magic. And he remembered the Patah, and how they had taught him how to read the stars in order to find himself beneath them; and the Boskiis, and how they'd taught him how to find direction in the delicious magic of nature.

"Katook?" said Quigga sleepily.

"You're tired," Katook said gently. "Try to go back to sleep."

"Will you do something for me?" Quigga's voice was more vulnerable than Katook had ever heard it.

"Anything."

"Teach me what the Patah taught you—how to read the stars. Perhaps if you do that, then I will find my way."

"Of course. Do you see that very bright one over there?"

"Yes, I think so." Quigga raised his head toward the horizon.

"Good, then follow it with your eyes to that sparkly blue star straight above it and slightly to the left . . . Look higher, no, higher!"

Quigga reared up, pawing at the spangled heavens. "Yes, I see it. I see it!"

"Of all the stars, that one never moves. It's always there," Katook told him softly. "If you find that star, you will always find your way."

Lost in the stars, Katook and Quigga stayed up very late that night. When they finally fell asleep, the sky was almost entirely drained of black and was flushed with blue. Katook dreamed of sapphire-blue butterflies passing across the moon on their way toward a range of distant, craggy mountains. He could see the mountains so clearly in his dream, every ridge, every valley, every silver trail of water. He marveled at how the tallest peak was shaped like a parrot's head, one side gently rounded, the other angled with a steeply sloping beak.

And Quigga dreamed of running with his herd again and the mindless delight of losing himself in a strong gallop.

159

The sun was shoulder-high when Quigga finally nuzzled Katook awake. "Get up. It's time to go."

"Where?" asked Katook groggily.

"That way," said Quigga with a surety Katook had never heard in his friend's voice. "I'm sure of it. It's that way." Quigga swung his head toward the wide plain.

Katook saw the sheer joy in Quigga's eyes. For the first time in his life, he sensed, Quigga knew exactly which way he should go.

"Quickly, climb onto my back!" Quigga said.

They raced arrowlike through the clear pastel light of dawn to an outcrop overlooking a valley. Quigga slid to an abrupt stop. There below them was an enormous herd of quaggas, kicking up golden dust as they galloped across the savanna.

"Look!" said Quigga, rearing up and joyously churning his forelegs in the air. "My herd!"

Katook felt proud and happy for Quigga, but as he looked about, his smile vanished. Off in the distance was a familiar mountain range, its tallest peak in the shape of a parrot's head. There was no doubt in Katook's mind: These were the same mountains he had seen in his dream the night before.

161

The mountains were to the north, but Quigga was pointing south.

"What's wrong?" asked Quigga, seeing the sadness wash over Katook's face.

"I dreamed of those mountains last night," answered Katook, pointing to the north. "The dream was so clear—that's my way. It's where I must go. And you've found *your* way." He pointed to the herd.

"But it can be your way, too," Quigga said. "You can ride on my back and live with us. We'll be your herd."

Tears flooded Katook's eyes, and he struggled for the right answer.

"Come with me," Quigga pleaded. "We'll be your family . . ."

But Katook knew better. He looked at Quigga and felt a deep, aching loss, knowing that they had come to the place where they must part.

"You're not coming with me, are you?" asked Quigga.

The two best friends gazed at each other. Both of them felt torn by grief. And yet each knew that he had to serve his own destiny—even if it meant going on without the other.

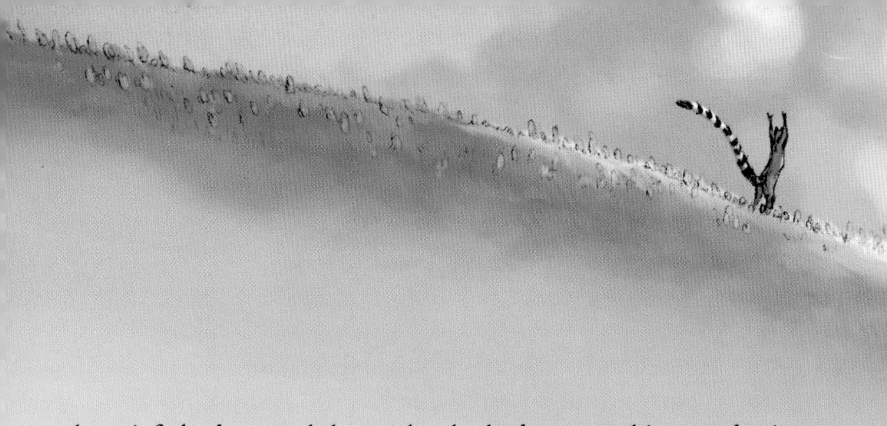

"I'll be fine" was Katook's only response.

"But—" said Quigga helplessly.

"Look at me and tell me that you doubt it," said Katook with a faint, forced smile.

Quigga saw the tears sliding down Katook's cheeks, but as he looked into Katook's eyes, he believed him. In his heart he knew that Katook would be fine.

Quigga pawed the earth. Then he whispered, "I will miss you."

"Not as much as I will miss you. Not by half." Katook choked back his tears. "Go now, hurry!"

Quigga nuzzled Katook's cheek.

"Good-bye, Quigga."

"Good-bye, Katook."

163

Chapter Eighteen
ALONE

Katook fought back tears as Quigga reluctantly turned away from him. He watched in silence as his friend slowly started down the long trail that zigzagged across the face of the plateau before it emptied onto the savanna below.

After a few moments he looked to the north, where he saw the advancing herd. He realized that if Quigga didn't hurry to meet them, they'd race past him without ever knowing he was there. And he knew that Quigga might never get another chance to find them.

"Hurry!" Katook yelled after his friend. "Run or you'll miss them!"

Quigga turned his great, wet eyes back at Katook.

"Run, Quigga!" cried Katook, feeling the tears starting to come again.

Quigga reared up and pawed the air, then galloped away, his mane whipping behind him and his legs stretching into long, graceful strides.

"That's right," said Katook softly to himself, then yelled, "Yes! Run!"

Even as he stood there, wishing for Quigga to rejoin his herd, Katook heard the whisper of fear and doubt playing inside his head. *Stop him!* it hissed. *Don't be a fool! You don't want to be left out here all by yourself. Think how lonely you'll be!* But Katook knew that though it hurt to watch his friend racing away, it was also right.

Katook saw Quigga reach the bottom of the cliffs and start galloping across the savanna toward his family. He stared with rapt awe, and just a touch of envy, as Quigga joined the herd and began running with them—hundreds of quaggas sprinting across the plain, moving as if they made up one wild, powerful, and beautiful animal.

They galloped past Katook, kicking up dust in their wake. The dust rose above them in a pale yellow mist that turned into a golden cloud so dense Katook lost sight of them.

At last Katook closed his eyes, aware that he was now more alone and unsure of his future than he'd been in all of his life. *There is no Nadab to find. No needle-guide. No map. No friend. There's no one to turn to, to find my way,* he thought.

He felt afraid to open his eyes. Afraid to turn around and face the uncertainty of what he might find in the mountains he'd seen in his dream the night before. He listened for the chirp or call of a bird just so that he wouldn't feel so alone. But he couldn't hear a thing.

I can't stand here forever, he finally admitted to himself, so he opened his eyes and turned toward the distant mountains. The dust hung heavy in the air. And for an instant, he saw the hazy shape of what looked vaguely like a lemur suspended only a couple of feet away. Then the dust swirled and the lemur became a cave and the cave became a tree, which became a river, and the river turned into a mountain. The amber-colored dust shifted from one image into another, on and on, until Katook lost all track of time.

Finally the dust twisted into a tight whirlwind that spun for a moment at Katook's feet, then seemed to melt into a small pool of golden light. Just as he was about to touch the shivering puddle of gold, it exploded. Katook jumped back, shielding his eyes. He felt a blast of warmth course through him, then heard a voice say, "Look at me, Katook."

He looked up and saw the Fossah. He was radiant in the sun, and his head was ringed with fire. His great eyes blazed, shifting endlessly between amber and blue.

Katook instantly dropped down and pressed his forehead into the dirt. Just as on Bo-hibba when the Fossah had appeared in the forest, he was filled with a terrifying wonder.

"Rise, Katook," said the Fossah in what the Boskiis had called *the voice at the heart of the world.* To Katook, it seemed to come from everywhere all at once.

Katook kept his eyes downcast as he slowly got to his feet. He was trembling, and the current in the air felt like that before a thunderstorm. Sweet. Alive. The ground he stood on seemed uncertain.

165

"Look at me," demanded the Fossah. "Do I frighten you?"

Shivering, Katook looked fully upon the Fossah.

And as his eyes met the Fossah's, his heart hammered in his chest.

Katook tried to speak, but found that he could not.

"Do I frighten you?" repeated the Fossah.

"N-no . . . no," replied Katook,

surprised to realize that this was the truth.

"Good. Come closer . . ."

Katook tentatively stepped forward until he was standing below
the Fossah, so close he could hear the Fossah's breathing. The sound
reminded him of the ocean. Just hearing it made him feel as if he were
back on the sea turtle again, far from shore, drifting peacefully under
the moonlit sky.

"Yes, I was there, too," said the Fossah, as if reading Katook's
thoughts. "And I was there in the look of wonder you saw in the Boskiis'
eyes, and in the wind, and the stars, and the river, and in the sapphire
butterflies, and in the joy of being with those you love and in the pain
of saying good-bye to them."

"I've known you," said Katook simply.

166

"Yes, you have. And I have always been before you, beside you, and behind you. I am, and have always been, with you. And you've come far and endured much to be here with me now," said the Fossah. "Look around you, Katook."

Katook pulled his gaze from the Fossah's and as he did, what he saw confused and amazed him. The plateau he had been standing on only seconds ago had vanished. In its place, for as far as Katook could see, was a land where predators and prey played together; where fruit grew fat and sweet on the trees and flowers never lost their bloom. And there were lemurs. They were everywhere, bounding through the trees, grooming each other in the warmth of the sun—

those who had been dead and those not yet born—and they gazed at Katook with welcome in their eyes.

At last, Katook thought. *At long last I've found home.*

"Yes, this is True Home," said the Fossah. "You will never be hungry here. You will never be lonely. And you can stay as long as you like."

Stunned, Katook asked softly, "Is this my reward for having come so far?"

167

The Fossah looked at Katook but was silent.

Confused, Katook glanced around his surroundings in wonder, thinking: *What a beautiful place. Of course I'll stay, how could I not?* But then just as he was about to say this aloud, he noticed a pond of indigo-black water that was swirling with liquid silver. He looked down into it and saw that the liquid silver was coming together on the surface of the water and as it did, it reflected back an image that dropped Katook to his knees. It was Kattakuk seen from high above.

"It's my village," murmured Katook.

The trees were still bare, and the skies were still gray and cold. Katook leaned over the pool and looked more closely at its reflected surface; he thought he could see the distant shapes of lemurs. They were clawing at the ground.

"What are they doing?" Katook asked.

"Digging for something to eat."

"But they're lemurs," said Katook. "Lemurs don't dig in the dirt."

"They do if they're starving to death."

For a long moment Katook was silent. Finally he asked what he was afraid to ask: "My family, are they still alive?"

"Yes."

"But they're starving, too. Aren't they?"

"Yes," said the Fossah quietly.

70

"Then what can I do? How can I help them?"
The Fossah looked Katook squarely in the eyes.
"I have to go back," said Katook.
"Even if it means that you might die in getting there?" asked the Fossah gently.
Katook looked into his eyes. "Yes."
"Even if it means you will be killed upon your arrival?"
Every bone in Katook's body wanted to scream, *I don't want to go. I want to stay here with you!* But somehow he knew that those words would never pass his lips.
"They will want to kill you," said the Fossah, very softly. "You frightened them. You know that, don't you?"
"I think so."
"Still, you would return to them?"
"Yes," said Katook very bravely.
"Aren't you frightened?"
"Very much," answered Katook. Then, with his voice quivering with wonder, he said, "I have to go. It's right."
The Fossah was silent a moment. Then he reached out and placed a tiny seed in Katook's paw. "Remember me in this," he said, and then as mysteriously as he had appeared from the cloud of dust, he slowly receded back into it, until he was gone.

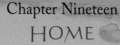

Chapter Nineteen
HOME

The seed was black and no bigger than a butterfly's eye, nothing more than a little dark speck in Katook's palm. He tucked it away in the pouch that hung from his neck. When he looked up again, he was no longer standing on the plateau where, moments earlier, the Fossah had appeared to him. Instead, he was on a familiar path under a cold gray sky with a freezing wind rippling through his fur.

Confused, Katook slowly turned in place. "It's impossible," he said aloud as he realized he now stood on the outskirts of Kattakuk. In fact, he was standing on exactly the same path he had traveled locked inside a cage on the back of a moa so many moon-treads ago.

He looked off toward the village in the distance and saw, through the cold mist falling around him, the gnarled shape of the ancient black baobab tree that was both temple and home of the High Priest. And beyond the temple, Katook saw the tiny silhouettes of basket homes hanging from the trees. He imagined his family huddled together inside theirs, silently waiting for the sky to break open. He wondered if he was too late; if they were already dead. But to reach home and find out, he'd first have to go past Gamic and his Indrii guards.

He looked up at the sky; it felt even heavier than he remembered, and the ground felt colder beneath his feet. There was no sign of life. Even the barren, stout-limbed trees were bent over as if in defeat. He reached for the pouch and felt the tiny seed inside it. It made no sense, but somehow this comforted Katook.

With his limbs shivering with fear and his ears twitching, searching for sounds of danger in the dark and freezing woods around him, Katook crept down the path toward home. Each step brought him closer to knowing if his family was dead or alive, and closer to his own death if Gamic found out that he'd returned.

He hadn't gone far before he saw an older female up ahead.

She was so thin it looked as if her fur was hanging on her bones. She was on her haunches digging in the ground for roots, frantically searching for food. As Katook got closer, he saw that her paws were raw and bleeding.

"Hello . . . ?" Katook called.

She froze a second, then continued digging. *Either she doesn't hear me, or she's afraid to look at me,* Katook thought.

"I won't hurt you," he said softly.

This time she turned very slowly, and he saw tears sliding down her hollow cheeks.

"Oh, my baby . . . ," she whispered. "My baby . . ."

Katook dropped to his knees beside her. "Mother . . . you're alive!"

Oola's only answer was to cry even harder. She was so frail, he was afraid he would crush her as he drew her gently into his chest. After a moment she pulled away and looked at her eldest son. "I didn't think I'd ever see you again," she whispered.

"I know . . . ," Katook answered, unable to say more because he, too, was crying.

She touched his cheek. "The priests told me you were dead."

"That's not the only lie that they've told," he managed to say. "Mother, I've seen so much—"

"But you're home now."

"Yes," he answered, and again held her close. He wanted to know about Kai and Lina and his father, but he was afraid to ask. Then he heard the sound of someone running toward them.

"Mother . . . ?" came a voice from the woods.

Katook turned and saw his little brother sprinting from the trees. Kai stumbled and fell. When he got to his feet,

Katook was shocked by how thin he was and how dull his once lustrous fur looked. But his eyes were still as bright as ever.

Kai ran straight into Katook's arms. "I don't believe it! Oh, it is . . . it is you! I knew you'd come back!"

Katook anxiously looked from his brother to his mother, and just as he gathered the courage to ask, "Lina and Father, are they—" Kai cut him off.

"Get up," he said, desperately trying to pull Katook to his feet. "We've got to get out of here before anyone sees you."

"Kai, I'm not going away again," said Katook, trying to sound sure of himself, though he felt far from it.

"You have to! If the Indriis find you here, they'll kill you. Please, Katook, I don't want you to die."

Katook looked to his mother, who was on her feet, offering her paw to help him up. "He's right," she said with a trembling voice. "Go. Go hide . . ."

"But—" Katook's voice froze in his throat as Reet stepped from the trees along with four other Indrii guards. Reet was thinner than Katook remembered, but that only made him appear more fierce and cruel. With a flick of his powerful wrist, Reet motioned to the other guards, who surrounded Katook, blocking his escape.

"If it isn't our blue-eyed castaway," said Reet with a vicious grin, seizing Katook by the scruff of his neck and holding him within inches of his face. "It will be my pleasure to hurt you."

"I haven't done anything wrong," said Katook, his voice quavering.

"You are here. That in itself is wrong." Reet shoved Katook back into the arms of the other guards. "Bring him."

"But my son . . . ," cried Oola. She grabbed Reet by his leg.

"Get off me!" He shook her off and sent her tumbling in the dirt. He stabbed his finger in the direction of Kai. "That's your son. Your *only* son. Don't make me take him, too." Then he started toward the center of Kattakuk, the guards hauling Katook after them.

The paths were empty, but Katook felt eyes watching him. He looked up toward the basket homes and saw flickers of movement. He knew that no one would dare try to stop Reet, for everyone on Bo-hibba was afraid of him, but they were terrified of Gamic.

Katook's heart hammered as they reached the temple.

Reet grabbed Katook by the neck, yanking him away from the guards.

"Go," he ordered them.

Reet waited until they were gone then rapped on the temple door. Two long *thuds*, one short one. The door slowly hinged open, and Reet shoved Katook through it.

In silence he led Katook up a steep, winding stairway inside the dead baobab tree. They stopped on a landing outside a door made of burned black wood. Reet lightly tapped on it then stood back and bowed his head. Katook knew who lived behind this door and silently prayed for it not to open.

His prayer was not answered. With a loud creak, the door opened and a slither of smoke wound its way onto the landing. Katook recognized the smell.

"Come," Gamic said softly from inside.

The High Priest's chamber was dimly lit and hazed with burning incense. Squinting in the dark, Katook saw stacks of large wicker baskets clustered around the chamber. He knew the baskets were used to collect offerings for the Fossah and wondered if they were empty or full.

"This time they're empty," a voice said from across the room.

Startled, Katook looked up. Flanked by other priests and a pair of Indrii guards, Gamic sat on a throne made from twisted, blackened fig branches.

174

"But it doesn't matter as far as you're concerned, does it?" Gamic's moon-yellow eyes burned from behind his ceremonial mask. "Full, empty, you'll not live long enough to concern yourself either way . . . On your knees," he commanded.

Katook, for a reason he couldn't explain, remained standing. The other priests gasped.

"You heard me," said Gamic in a voice barely louder than a whisper. "On your knees and prepare to receive the Fossah's judgment."

Katook's entire body shivered with fear, but he refused to kneel before the High Priest. He stammered, "All I w-want is to live here again. Please, that's all I want. I won't cause you any—"

Gamic stretched out one emaciated hand. "Reet!"

The guard reached up and forced the little lemur's face into the floor.

"I call upon you, great Fossah," screamed Gamic, "to grant me the power to punish this outcast!"

While Reet and the other guards kept their eyes fixed on the ground, Katook stole a glance upward and saw Gamic reach into two small gourds hidden under his throne at his feet.

"Oh, great Fossah, shall I speak for you?" Gamic called out. Then, with a flamboyant wave of his arms, he flared his fingers; ice-blue sparks crackled over his head and fell softly all around him.

Katook saw the fear and awe in Reet and the other Indriis. "He speaks for the Fossah," they murmured softly. But he also recalled the Patah and their magic lantern show and the powders they used. He remembered Hasara explaining how each powder was harmless on its own, and only revealed its magic when mixed with the other. *This is how he rules them*, thought Katook. *This is how he ruled us all—through trickery, not through the Fossah's true power.*

Gamic slowly rose from his throne. Approaching Katook on his weak and spindly legs, he tripped stepping down from the small dais. Katook leapt to his feet and caught Gamic by the arm, their eyes locked. In that instant Katook thought he saw shock in Gamic's eyes.

But Gamic quickly looked away.

"The Fossah is kind," Katook said to him quietly.

"*You* speak of the great Fossah? An outcast! Still your tongue or I will have it torn from your head!"

"He's gentle. And he wishes me no harm for returning to my home. He sent me here."

"On your knees!" yelled Gamic hysterically. "Get down on your knees or I will take your life here and now!"

Gamic's thin body trembled with barely contained rage. Katook knew he should be afraid, but he felt more pity for Gamic than fear for his own life.

The guards stared at Katook with amazement. They had never seen anyone defy their master. Their haunches twitched. Then they sprang to force Katook to his knees.

Katook bolted past them. He burst through a pile of baskets, then vanished under Gamic's throne. He found the gourds hidden there, grabbed two pawfuls of powder, and clenched his fists just as the guards got hold of his feet and dragged him out. They threw him to the ground in front of Gamic.

"Take this—this liar and silence him, once and for all!" Gamic screamed.

Katook looked through Gamic's mask and into the wild rage of the High Priest's eyes. "I've done nothing wrong, Gamic. You know this."

Gamic stared down at him.

"You do," Katook went on. "You know it in your heart."

A breeze rustled through Gamic's cape as the Indriis stood mesmerized by the certainty in the young lemur's blue eyes.

"Leave us," Gamic said finally, his voice hoarse with emotion. When he and Katook were alone in the chamber, he whispered, "What do you know of the Fossah?"

"I've seen him."

Gamic's long, slender fingers splayed open again and again as he gazed at Katook.

"You don't believe me, do you?"

"It is just you and me here now," began Gamic in a quiet, oddly weary voice. "I've spent every waking hour of every

176

day of my life serving the Fossah. I've devoted *everything* to him. And I would willingly sacrifice anything to be closer to him." His voice rose in anger and frustration. "But *you*—you who are nothing more than a common kit—have seen what I yearned for my whole life. Yes, I believe you. I believe that for a reason I don't understand, that I may *never* understand, you were shown what was meant for *me* to see."

"I didn't ask for this," Katook said quietly.

"Nor did I." And with that, Gamic pulled open the door to reveal the waiting Indriis. "Kill him."

Reet yanked Katook out of the High Priest's chamber, sending him sprawling across the landing. Digging his claws into Katook's forearm, he jerked him to his feet and dragged him toward the stairs. Gamic's guards followed, descending inside the petrified baobab tree to the place below the tree's twisted, long-dead roots where lives were taken.

Katook walked bravely with his executioners. "Reet, just for a moment, will you listen to me?" he asked.

"Silence!"

"I know it's forbidden to disobey Gamic," Katook went on, "but he's confused."

"I said, silence!"

But Katook continued calmly, "And to disregard the instructions of someone whose mind is as muddled as his, isn't just the right thing to do, it's the only thing to do."

"I have my orders," Reet insisted.

"You have flawed *instructions*."

Suddenly Reet shoved Katook into the wall, "And *you* can tell the difference?"

"Yes. Yes, I can. So can you."

With his eyes locked on Katook, Reet dashed him to the ground. Blood gushed from Katook's nose. His eyes blurred.

Katook struggled to his feet. "Kill me, if you will, but believe me when I tell you that Gamic doesn't speak for the Fossah."

And with that, Katook flung his arms into the air and released the two powders he had taken from Gamic's chamber. Blue sparks flared brightly overhead. Reet and the other guards instantly dropped to their knees. Averting their eyes as the flakes of blue sparks fell all around them, they murmured in unison, "He speaks for the Fossah."

Katook knelt beside Reet and said, "Look at me."

But the Indrii guard kept his eyes fixed on the floor.

"Please . . . ?" said Katook very gently. "Look at me."

Slowly Reet turned his gaze toward him.

"I've been afraid of you since I was a kit," Katook began. "Everyone in Kattakuk is afraid of you. But that's not what I want from you. Don't you think we've had enough fear in this village?"

Reet didn't respond, and Katook knew he had to try again. "There's no reason to be afraid of me," he said.

Reet was silent a moment; then he got to his feet and spoke softly. "Release him."

Reet and the other guards accompanied Katook through the deserted village. They walked out past the farthest marker at the edge of town, where they awaited his orders.

"Thank you" was all Katook said.

Reet shuffled from one foot to the other, hesitant to leave Katook there by himself.

"I'll be fine," said Katook, answering Reet's unasked question. "Now go. Before you all get in trouble."

Katook watched them walk away. He looked up toward his family's home in the distance and imagined himself snuggled inside, Kai on one side of him, Lina on the other, his father and mother sleeping peacefully, knowing that their son had finally returned. But Katook knew that if he ever went there again, he would jeopardize their safety.

It was almost dark. Icy winds bit at him. He hoped to find shelter in a tree, but there weren't any trees this far from town. Katook closed his eyes, half expecting that when he opened them he'd be back with the Fossah. But the sky was only darker.

No, he thought, no more running. *If I'm going to die, at least I'll die here, close to my family.*

Alone, cold, and hungry, Katook curled up against the side of a boulder and fell into a deep sleep. He slept tightly clutching the bag that held the seed the Fossah had given him. He slept so soundly that he didn't even wake when a freezing rain began to fall.

Perhaps when he fell asleep there was already a cleft in the ground exactly beneath the tiny bag in Katook's paws, but I do not think so. And perhaps Katook's paws loosened as slumber relaxed his body, but I doubt that, too. Nevertheless, during the night, the seed spilled from Katook's pouch. It fell perfectly into the ground and was moistened by the rain. And its hard black sheath cracked open and tiny, fingerling tendrils of green slipped into the moist ground and found their heaven there.

Katook woke sheltered under the canopy of an enormous fig tree, its thick branches arcing over him, leaves bright green, backlit by a sun that burned brightly overhead. *I'm dreaming,* he thought. *This is just a dream.* He looked past the tree and saw that the freezing rain was falling just beyond it. "Impossible," he said aloud.

Then he saw the figs. They were everywhere. Dripping from the branches like enormous, purple-black raindrops; their sweet swollen bellies so heavy, they looked as if they would drop from the tree with the slightest breeze. Hundreds, no, thousands of them. Each more perfect than the next. Katook gave a fig a gentle tug, closed his eyes, and gave thanks.

Gamic woke in a foul mood from a horrible night's rest. He'd dreamed that Katook sat on the side of his bed watching him sleep. He hated the expression on Katook's face—so peaceful, without fear or blame.

"Forget him, he is no longer," Gamic muttered to himself as he walked to his window. He knew the view would calm him, it always did. But that day, as he gazed out across Kattakuk, he saw for the first time in a long, long time, plump, bright drops of rain falling from the sky. Then through the wash of rain, Gamic noticed something that took his breath away.

On the very edge of the village, glowing in a beam of bright light that plunged through a fissure in the gray-black sky, was the most enormous fig tree Gamic had ever seen. Even from this distance, Gamic could see the figs, like hundreds of dark birds finding shade under sun-drenched wide green leaves. And climbing in this most magnificent of trees was Katook, his fur glistening in the sunlight.

"It can't be," Gamic said to himself.

All of Kattakuk was still asleep as Gamic, wearing his ceremonial finest, passed through the village, heading toward the miraculous tree. Moments later the High Priest stood in the circle of warm sunlight. The sun, the tree—they were both as real as his own paws.

He craned his neck and saw Katook in the uppermost limbs. The young lemur was carefully picking figs and laying them in a basket he'd woven out of slender fig branches and lined with lush green leaves. Sensing Gamic standing there, Katook looked down.

"You must be hungry," said Katook.

"Yes," whispered Gamic, almost too stunned to speak.

Katook climbed down. He picked out a particularly fat and juicy fig from his basket and offered it to Gamic. "Here . . . try this one."

But Gamic didn't take the fig. Instead he knelt down in front of Katook and said in a voice full of misery, "I'm not worthy." Slowly he removed his mask and revealed his face for the first time. He was crying.

"Please, don't," said Katook, helping the High Priest to his feet, but Gamic refused to be comforted. As he covered his face with his paws, Katook put his arm around Gamic's narrow shoulders. "Then I'll sit with you," said Katook. "And we'll admire this beautiful tree together."

After a while Katook rose and offered his paw to Gamic. "Will you help me?" asked Katook.

"Yes," replied Gamic, "I will help you."

And he did. Together they made more baskets, then picked every ripe fruit on that impossible tree. As they were about to start carrying the heavy baskets back into the village, Gamic handed Katook his cape and mask.

"You should wear these, not I," he said.

Katook studied the severe expression carved into the mask and set it at the base of the tree.

"Then you at least must wear the cape," Gamic insisted.

"No," Katook said, "we'll wear it together." He snapped it open and pulled it around their shoulders. But as they started walking away from the tree and toward the freezing rain that fell just beyond it, the warm circle of sunlight widened to include them, and the farther they walked from the fig tree, the wider the circle became.

Katook looked up at the blue sky. "Well, I guess we won't need this after all."

Gamic nodded, and Katook set the purple cape down on the ground.

Then he and Katook, walking side by side, carried the heavy baskets of figs into the village. As they walked, the sky turned clear overhead and the sun shone bright on their backs, warming them to their very core.

With the sun in his face, Katook sprawled on a bed of thick green grass. Above him was a familiar fig tree, heavy with swollen fruit. And way, way up in the tree, shaded by wide, gold-veined leaves, Kai and Lina were laughing and gorging themselves. Drowsy, Katook felt the warm grass on his cheek. He looked over at his mother, drifting off to sleep in his father's arms. And he suddenly realized that he had been here before in what he thought was a dream but now recognized as a foretelling. He was, at long last, home.

Epilogue

"And that," the storyteller said, "is the story of how Katook brought an end to the Long Winter." With that, the elderly lemur slowly rose from the warm branch he was lounging on and started climbing back down the tree.

The young lemurs followed him eagerly. Though the sun was beginning to set, and it was time for them to return to their homes, they clustered around him.

"But then what?" one of them asked. "What happened to Katook?"

"And Quigga?" asked another. "Did Katook ever see him again?"

The storyteller smiled mischievously but continued moving toward the baskets of fruit that awaited him in the cool shade of the baobab tree.

"At least tell us, was Gamic really Katook's friend, or was he faking it so he could kill him later?"

The storyteller looked at the curious young kits. "I will tell you this. Gamic found what he had lost. And Katook and Quigga both had many more adventures, though whether they had them alone or together, I won't say."

"Why not?" demanded one of the young ones. "We'll be as silent as the sun."

The storyteller smiled, and patted the young lemur on his furry little head. "Because that, my young friends, is a story for another day."

For my husband
—Terryl Whitlatch

Grateful thanks and heartfelt appreciation to my husband, Tom; Robert Gould; David Wieger; Ellen Steiber; Stephanie Lostimolo; Jake Lebovic; Lisa Larson; Westminster Presbyterian Church; Jeff Johnson and Ark Music; Muriel Nellis at LCA; the good folks at Simon & Schuster, especially Walter Weintz, Ruth Fecych, and Peter McCulloch; and my parents, Joan and Larry Martens, without whose faith, hard work, and prayers this endeavor would not have been possible.

SOLIS DEO GLORIA

Join the adventure!
Visit the official Katurran Odyssey™ website:
www.katurranodyssey.com

An Imaginosis Book
www.imaginosis.com

Design and art direction by Robert Gould / Imaginosis
Graphic design by Jake Lebovic
Title logo design by Stephanie Lostimolo

Digital scanning by Powerhouse, LA
Created and designed on Macintosh computers

Dedicated to the children of my life: Adducci, Tessapuna, J-Man, Coop-Daddy, Sophie-Girl, Dia "The Neck," Matecki-Man, and Sydaluna
—David Michael Wieger

I'd like to thank Robert Gould for being a fierce advocate, a great friend, and an insightful alchemist. Thank you to Ellen Steiber for making me a better writer. To my family and friends for their love, support, but most of all for putting up with me. And I'd like to thank my wife, Saral, for guiding my heart to places it had never been before.

SIMON & SCHUSTER
Rockefeller Center
1230 Avenue of the Americas
New York, NY 10020

For information regarding special discounts for bulk purchases, please contact Simon & Schuster Special Sales at 1-800-456-6798 or business@simonandschuster.com

Manufactured in Italy

10 9 8 7 6 5 4 3 2 1

ISBN 0-7432-2500-7

AZULD
NARRAGON
(WINTER SEA)

NAKU

SKAG

DALEE

BEHNAK WASTE

NARGAD EAT

NARRAGIZ WASTE

YIGRRIDD

BUNDA-MAAR

BUNDA-BIKU

ISNAIR

SEA OF NARSID

AZULD OCCIPITA (AUTUMN SEA)

BOGS

GOROKA STEPPES

OOUNDAMAR

TULI

BEORIKIVI

BWYD-TORR

GWOOUNDAMAR

AGGOLA HOLD

SAGIZA

ALTA-LAYA

ALTAGORNAN R.

JUDGEMENT DELLS

KOLLOBASSA

THE GREAT PATAH DESERT (S'ARIR)

BOSKII RAINFOREST (NATEESK)

HATIPHA HOLD

BA-OO-IAG

CRRIZZIG-FEEG

RIBCAGE ARCHES

TOOFA SEA

GEELONG R.

ACCO HARBOR

ACCO

BITURRONGO BAY

GEEBAN'S WASTE

THE DEAD CITY

DUNES

SPLESHAG MARSH

GABADDON'S END (SHORE OF EXILE)

KBBBI-JINN

BEEHIVE PINNACLES

TA'IZZ

GEELONG DELTA

GEELONG FALLS

JALINGO GULF

SU

B

OBSI-BAB

KATTAKUK

BOHIBBAH

S'ARIR PAN

JALINGO TROPICS

KA-SHAB ISLANDS

JALINGO ISLANDS

A MAP of the
CENTRAL CONTINENTS
of
KATURRAH

AZULD NIANNA
(SUMMER SEA)

CIANNARETH

CIANNA